The Mermaid COLE

AN ENTERTAINMENT
BASED ON THE WORDS AND MUSIC OF
COLE PORTER

DEVISED BY
ALAN STRACHAN
BENNY GREEN

> COLE may only be performed in the format presented in this acting edition, and under no circumstances may any alterations be made, or substitution of other Cole Porter material.

SAMUEL FRENCH, INC.
45 WEST 25TH STREET   NEW YORK 10010
7623 SUNSET BOULEVARD   HOLLYWOOD 90046
LONDON   *TORONTO*

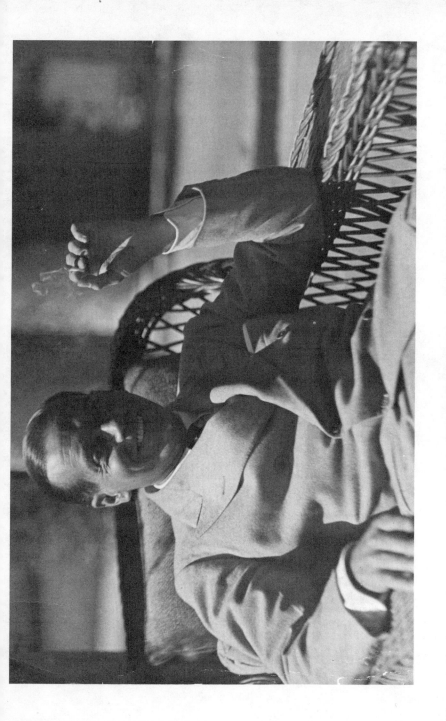

Even this late in the day, comparatively few people realise, I think, the extent to which an independent income can affect the way a man resolves a dominant seventh chord. The oversight on the public's part is doubly surprising in view of the fact that an extremely intricate and sophisticated scientific instrument exists for measuring the interaction between music and money. This instrument is called the human ear, and to that fortunate minority of my readers who possess one, or, in a few special cases, a pair, it will have been apparent to them that the music of Mendelssohn was composed by a much richer gentleman than, say, the one who wrote Wagner's operas.

The same is true of Cole Porter, whose life, to say nothing of his life-style, made a sorry mess of the old pulp-press platitude that great songwriters are necessarily born in crapulous tenements, among relatives who think that alliteration is something to do with eating too many radishes. That scenario was true enough in the cases of George Gershwin and Irving Berlin, but it had nothing remotely to do with either Jerome Kern or Richard Rodgers, both of whom were satisfied sons of the middle-class. But most of all, the tenement syndrome had absolutely nothing to do with Cole Porter.

There are those who are bewildered by the fact that a man who has no economic need to work should work as hard as Porter did. The explanation is so elementary that I blush to put it on paper. Porter laboured as ceaselessly as he did because like all first-rate creative workers he couldn't help himself. The urge to write songs like "I Get a Kick Out of You" is unrelated to anything except itself, and the categorical imperative which pushed Porter to the hair-raising drudgery of twenty-six musical comedies was neither dreams of avarice nor vaulting ambition nor thoughts of posterity's plaudits, but simply the intense sensation of fulfilment a man experiences when, having wandered for the thousandth time down the corridors of his own mind, he comes up with a scheme to make the tonality of his melody change at the point in the lyrical story where the words go

There's no love song finer,
but how strange
the change
from major to minor.

How much money is such a scheme worth? The moment we pose the question we realise the lunacy of trying to answer it, and how idiotic a theory it is that people only do things for money. And just to underline the point, Porter actually slaved at two men's jobs. Like the thespian who made sure of the reviews by playing Iago *and* Othello, Porter did things, not by halves, but by doubles. For instance he attended both Yale and Harvard, a bizarre educational process subsidised by the rich grandfather who insisted on it. Later Porter spent the postwar years moving from one European playground to another, privately fretting over the fact that the dullards of Broadway hardly took him seriously. By the time he was ready to knock everybody silly in 1928 with shows whose scores included "Let's Do it" and "You Do Something

To Me," he was already in his mid-thirties, a freakishly venerable age for a songwriter to arrive. At 35 Berlin had already had two and a half careers, Rodgers had completed almost the entire oeuvre of the Lorenz Hart musicals, and Gershwin's life was almost over.

There is no question that Porter delayed his entry because he was rich enough to afford to take his time. But there is no question either that the money which tempted him to spend so long splashing in the pools of the Côte d'Azur, gave to his work a kind of plutocratic stylishness which distinguishes it from the work of all his contemporaries. Porter wrote affluent music, and the affluence is more than just a question of the catalogue of expensive hedonism which may be found in a song like "At Long Last Love." The elegance of his musical cadences, even in an apparent flippant trifle like "Goodbye Little Dream," where in the twenty-first and twenty-second bars the melody climbs on the underpinning of an archetypal Porter harmonic progression, the frequent suave insolence of his rhymes, as in "The Leader of a Big Time Band," where he raises a laugh through the comical inversion of describing a stripper so confused that she puts her clothes *on*, the fearless flouting of the 32-bar unwritten rule in songs like "Night and Day," "Begin the Beguine," "Just One of Those Things," the derisive reduction of John the Baptist to "John the B," the apparent wrapping up of the middle eight passage of "Love for Sale," followed by a brilliant further development which turns the sequence into a middle sixteen, these and a thousand other facets point to the kind of insouciance a man usually possesses only when his bank manager defers to him. Probably the difference between a masterpiece like Porter's "It's All Right With Me" and a masterpiece like Berlin's "I'm Putting All My Eggs in One Basket" is that while Porter snapped his fingers at waiters, Berlin actually was one.

Mention of "It's All Right With Me" raises the question of words-and-music. In the rare case of a man who does both, which comes first? The answer to that question provided by the script of "Cole" is "Yes," and it is an answer meant in all seriousness. From the technical point of view, Porter's best work is fascinating because of the insistent inference in passage after passage after passage, that the choicest phrases, musically as well as lyrically speaking, sprang to mind as part of a whole. In "It's All Right With Me," two short melodic phrases are followed by one extended variation upon them, a musical motif which Porter used time and time again. Matching these phrases is a rhyme scheme based on the device of the repetition of the same adjective (in the first section, "wrong") three times, the rhyme itself coming with the second and third of the nouns qualified by the adjective. This kind of marriage of the verbal and melodic idea is possible when two writers are involved, but only just. To Porter it appears to have been instinctive, and the fact that he was aware of the incalculable benefits of the double nature of his talent is suggested by his affected surprise, when confronted by a Rodgers-and-Hammerstein hit, that it should take *two* men to write one song.

In artistic terms Porter was, like most of his contemporaries, an offshoot of that benevolent curmudgeon, W. S. Gilbert. The other rhymster's name to occur in the Porter chronicles is that of Robert Browning, and it is somehow the last word on Porter's curious compromise between sybaritism and artistic dedication that whereas you and I, besotted with Browning's technique, might be impelled to go and take a look at the Venetian palazzo where Browning once lived, Porter went and rented it. He was a man so meticulous in his craft that even the apparent trifles are beautifully wrought. He wrote no slovenly songs that I know of, was a master of pastiche (witness the delicious overripe aroma of his Bowery waltz, "Brush Up Your Shakespeare"), and was, in his finest moments, which were many, a wit and a sympathetic chronicler of that agonising psychic ordeal usually referred to as Love. He is already a classic, and one day will be seen as one of the most charming, skilful and civilised reporters of that astonishing spectacle, the twentieth century in mid-flight.

Benny Green

Applications for STOCK, REPERTORY or AMATEUR performances of COLE in any part of the world must be made to SAMUEL FRENCH INC. at one of the following addresses:

Samuel French Inc
45 West 25th Street
New York, N.Y. 10010
Tel: (212) 582 4700

Samuel French (Canada) Ltd
80 Richmond Street East
Toronto, Ontario M5C 1P1 CANADA
Tel: (416) 363 3536

Samuel French Ltd
26 Southampton Street
Strand
London WC2, ENGLAND
Tel: (O1) 836 7513

Dominie Property Ltd
8 Cross Street
Brookvale, Sydney, NSW
AUSTRALIA
Tel: (2) 93 0201

FOR ALL RIGHTS OTHER THAN THOSE STIPULATED ABOVE, APPLICATION MUST BE MADE TO ONE OF THE COPYRIGHT OWNERS AT THE FOLLOWING ADDRESSES:

COLE PORTER MUSICAL AND LITERARY PROPERTY TRUSTS
345 Park Avenue, New York, N.Y. 10154
Tel: (212) 644-8622   Telex: 666843

DEREK GLYNNE, LONDON COMPANY (International Plays) Ltd
25 Haymarket, London SW1Y 4EN ENGLAND   Tel: (01) 930 1981
Cables: INTERPLAY LONDON   Telex: 919150 MANOAH G

WARNING: The publication of this work in any acting edition, collection of songs, vocal score or album either in the USA, the British Commonwealth, the Dominion of Canada, or elsewhere throughout the world must not be taken to imply that it is necessarily available for performance by amateurs or professionals either in the USA, Great Britain or elsewhere throughout the world before application for licence has been made and obtained.

The Copyright Owners of the stage entertainment COLE are: THE MERMAID THEATRE TRUST, THE COLE PORTER MUSICAL AND LITERARY PROPERTY TRUSTS, DEREK GLYNNE, and THE LONDON COMPANY (International Plays) Ltd.

© 1981

Orchestrations © 1981 by THE LONDON COMPANY (International Plays) Ltd and KENNETH MOULE.

COLE is fully protected under the copyright laws of the British Commonwealth of Nations, the United States of America, and all other countries of the Berne and Universal Copyright Conventions.

ACKNOWLEDGMENTS

The following songs© Chappell & Co. Inc., year indicated:
  WHEN LOVE BECKONED (ON FIFTY-SECOND STREET)© 1939
  DOWN IN THE DEPTHS (ON THE NINETIETH FLOOR)© 1936
  TOMORROW © 1938
  AT LONG LAST LOVE © 1937
  IT'S DE-LOVELY © 1936
  MAKE IT ANOTHER OLD-FASHIONED PLEASE © 1940
  MOST GENTLEMEN DON'T LIKE LOVE © 1938
  THE LEADER OF A BIG-TIME BAND © 1943
  EV'RY TIME WE SAY GOODBYE © 1944
The followings songs © Metro-Goldwyn-Mayer Corp.:
  IN THE STILL OF THE NIGHT © 1937
The following song © Loew's Inc.:
  BE A CLOWN © 1946
  PLEASE DON'T MONKEY WITH BROADWAY © 1939
  I CONCENTRATE ON YOU © 1939
The following song © Robert H. Montgomery, Jr., Trustee:
  BIG TOWN © 1980
The following songs © John F. Wharton, as Trustee:
  WHEN THE SUMMER MOON COMES 'LONG © 1974
  DIZZY BABY © 1966
  WITHIN THE QUOTA © 1970
The followings songs © Cole Porter:
  WOULDN'T IT BE FUN © 1958
  ANOTHER OP'NIN, ANOTHER SHOW © 1949
  I LOVE PARIS © 1952
  THE LAZIEST GAL IN TOWN © 1927
  IT'S ALL RIGHT WITH ME © 1953
  WE SHALL NEVER BE YOUNGER © 1955
  WHY CAN'T YOU BEHAVE © 1948
  BRUSH UP YOUR SHAKESPEARE © 1949
  FROM THIS MOMENT ON © 1950

The following song © G. Schirmer:
  SEE AMERICA FIRST © 1916
The following song © Jerome H. Remick & Co.:
  BINGO ELI YALE © 1910
The following songs © M. E. Sayag:
  LOST LIBERTY BLUES © 1928
  DO YOU WANT TO SEE PARIS? © 1928
    (OMNIBUS)
The following songs © Harms, Inc.
  THANK YOU SO MUCH MISSUS LOWSBOROUGH—GOODBY © 1934
  YOU DON'T KNOW PAREE © 1929
  TAKE ME BACK TO MANHATTAN © 1930
  I HAPPEN TO LIKE NEW YORK © 1931
  I'M A GIGOLO © 1929
  LOVE FOR SALE © 1930
  NIGHT AND DAY © 1932
  ANYTHING GOES © 1934
  I GET A KICK OUT OF YOU © 1934
  WHAT IS THIS THING CALLED LOVE © 1929
  YOU DO SOMETHING TO ME © 1929
  YOU'VE GOT THAT THING © 1929
  LET'S MISBEHAVE © 1927
  I WORSHIP YOU © 1929
  JUST ONE OF THOSE THINGS © 1935
  BEGIN THE BEGUINE © 1935

CREDITS

Extract from Calvin Tomkins' LIVING WELL IS THE BEST REVENGE published in the United States of America by Avon, Copyright © 1971 by Calvin Tomkins.

Extracts from MY LOST CITY by F Scott Fitzgerald, © 1945 by New Directions (Copyright renewed).

Extract from ECHOES OF THE JAZZ AGE by F Scott Fitzgerald, © 1931 by Charles Scribner's Sons, renewed 1958 by Francis Scott Fitzgerald Lanahan.

Extract from SAVE ME THE WALTZ by Zelda Fitzgerald, © 1932 by Charles Scribner's Sons renewed 1960 by Francis Scott Fitzgerald Lanahan.

Fitzgerald extracts by permission of Laurence Pollinger Ltd and Harold Ober Associates Inc.

ISBN 0 573 68135 X

COLE was first produced at the Mermaid Theatre, London, on Tuesday 2 July 1974.

Founders and Artistic Directors: Lord Bernard Miles, CBE
Josephine Wilson

ORIGINAL CAST

RAY CORNELL

LUCY FENWICK

PETER GALE

BILL KERR

JULIA MCKENZIE

ROD MCLENNAN

KENNETH NELSON

ELIZABETH POWER

ANGELA RICHARDS

UNA STUBBS

Directed by ALAN STRACHAN and DAVID TOGURI
Designed by PETER DOCHERTY
Music arranged by KEN MOULE
Musical Director JOHN BURROWS
Lighting Designed by NICK CHELTON

Original Cast Album on RCA, RED SEAL Ser No LRL2 5054, Musical Score produced by SAMUEL FRENCH INC.

> **WARNING**
>
> Publication of this play does not imply it is available for performance. Please do not consider a production before permission is granted. Apply to Samuel French Ltd, 52 Fitzroy St., London W1P 6JR. Performance without permission is an infringement of copyright.

COLE ON STAGE

by ALAN STRACHAN

Cole was a long time in the making; the original idea developed from the success of *Cowardy Custard* which also began its life at the Mermaid, but it was clear from the outset that to attempt a carbon-copy of the Coward show or to follow the same formula exactly would be an unadventurous and somewhat profitless exercise. In this, luckily, we had full encouragement from Sir Bernard Miles, the Mermaid's Artistic Director who did not blanch even when it became apparent that *Cole* would be an expensive show for a small theatre to present.

Nevertheless, comparisons between the two shows, although odious, were inevitable. And indeed, the two composers, two of the undisputed giants of twentieth century popular music, share certain fascinating similarities. Both were darlings of the international cosmopolitan set of the between-the-war years, arch-sophisticates who yet managed to capture the popular imagination. Their images have in common a polished tuxedoed brilliance, but in both cases the origins are somewhat at odds with this image. Coward came from the shabby-gentility of Edwardian suburbia and Porter (although his background was without the poverty that haunted Coward's) emerged from the hinterlands of the American Puritan mid-West.

It is precisely this tension between the background and the later glamorous world into which they moved which gives the music and lyrics of both their particular resonance.

The Mermaid, with the invaluable co-operation of the Cole Porter Trusts, had been granted access to all Porter's songs, published and unpublished (with the exception of the songs from "Nymph Errant," previously optioned for a Broadway revival) so the main problem on the musical side—admittedly a huge one—was what to leave out. Working on the principle that if you try to please everybody you end up by pleasing nobody, we decided to attempt to illustrate the different facets of the unique Porter talent through the various sequences in the show and to strike some reasonable balance between the classic songs and those neglected or less familiar. Everybody is sure to have at least one favourite that is not included, but then to have included everything would have meant asking an audience to sit in the theatre for rather an unrealistically long time.

With *Cowardy Custard*, of course, the devising process was considerably helped by the wealth of linking material by Coward himself—plays, autobiographies, poems—to provide the thread with which to link the numbers. Porter, however, provided Benny Green and myself with no such convenient treasure-trove and the show's format finally resolved itself with a mixture of original narration and related extracts from Scott and Zelda Fitzgerald linking the songs, counterpointed with a constantly changing visual background whereby designer Peter Docherty and lighting designer Nick Chelton made superb use of back projection and the Mermaid's wide open stage.

CONTENTS

COLE is divided into the following sequences:

PART ONE

INTRODUCING COLE PORTER
YALE
PARIS
MANHATTAN
BROADWAY

PART TWO

WHAT IS THIS THING CALLED LOVE?
HOLLYWOOD
BACK TO BROADWAY
FINALE

There is no single NARRATOR figure. The various passages of narration and the extracts from Calvin Tomkins, and Scott and Zelda Fitzgerald are shared amongst the various members of the Company.

MUSICAL NUMBERS

PART ONE

OVERTURE
WOULDN'T IT BE FUN? ("Aladdin," TV show, 1958)
ANOTHER OP'NIN', ANOTHER SHOW ("Kiss Me Kate," 1948)
THE BOBOLINK WALTZ (1902)
BINGO ELI YALE! (Yale, 1910)
WHEN THE SUMMER MOON COMES 'LONG (Yale, 1910)
SEE AMERICA FIRST ("See America First," 1916)
LOST LIBERTY BLUES ("La Revue des Ambassadeurs," 1928)
I LOVE PARIS ("Can-Can," 1953)
DO YOU WANT TO SEE PARIS? ("Fifty Million Frenchmen," 1929)
MRS LOWSBOROUGH-GOODBY (Incidental song, 1934)
Extract from ballet WITHIN THE QUOTA (1923)
DIZZY BABY (Unused, "Paris," 1928)
YOU DON'T KNOW PAREE ("Fifty Million Frenchmen," 1929)
TAKE ME BACK TO MANHATTAN ("The New Yorkers," 1930)
I HAPPEN TO LIKE NEW YORK ("The New Yorkers," 1930)
BIG TOWN ("Seven Lively Arts," 1944)
I'M A GIGOLO ("Wake Up and Dream," 1929)
LOVE FOR SALE ("The New Yorkers")
WHEN LOVE BECKONED ON 52nd STREET ("Dubarry Was a Lady," 1939)
DOWN IN THE DEPTHS ("Red, Hot and Blue," 1936)
COME ON IN ("DuBarry Was a Lady," 1939)
NIGHT AND DAY ("Gay Divorce," 1932)
ANYTHING GOES ("Anything Goes," 1934)
I GET A KICK OUT OF YOU ("Anything Goes," 1934)
TOMORROW ("Leave It To Me," 1938)
TOMORROW (reprise)

INTERMISSION

PART TWO

ENTR'ACTE
BEGIN THE BEGUINE ("Jubilee," 1935)
WHAT IS THIS THING CALLED LOVE? ("Wake Up And Dream," 1929)
YOU DO SOMETHING TO ME ("Fifty Million Frenchmen," 1929)
YOU'VE GOT THAT THING ("Fifty Million Frenchmen")
LET'S MISBEHAVE (Unused, "Paris," 1928)
THE LAZIEST GAL IN TOWN (Written 1927, used in film "Stagefright," 1950)

AT LONG LAST LOVE ("You Never Know," 1938)
IT'S DE-LOVELY ("Red, Hot and Blue," 1936)
IN THE STILL OF THE NIGHT (Film "Rosalie," 1937)
I WORSHIP YOU (Unused "Fifty Million Frenchmen," 1929)
MAKE IT ANOTHER OLD-FASHIONED, PLEASE ("Panama Hattie," 1940)
MOST GENTLEMEN DON'T LIKE LOVE ("Leave It To Me," 1938)
IT'S ALL RIGHT WITH ME ("Can-Can," 1953)
FROM THIS MOMENT ON ("Kiss Me Kate" (film), 1953)
JUST ONE OF THOSE THINGS ("Jubilee," 1935)
WE SHALL NEVER BE YOUNGER (Unused, "Kiss Me Kate," 1948)
I CONCENTRATE ON YOU ("Broadway Melody of 1940")
WHAT IS THIS THING CALLED LOVE? (reprise)
BE A CLOWN (film, "The Pirate," 1948)
PLEASE DON'T MONKEY WITH BROADWAY (film, "Broadway Melody of 1940")
THE LEADER OF A BIG-TIME BAND ("Something For the Boys," 1943)
BRUSH UP YOUR SHAKESPEARE ("Kiss Me Kate," 1948)
WHY CAN'T YOU BEHAVE? ("Kiss Me Kate")
WOULDN'T IT BE FUN? (reprise)
EV'RY TIME WE SAY GOODBYE ("Seven Lively Arts," 1944)

Cole

PART ONE

A) INTRODUCING COLE PORTER

(*"Cole Porter" signature on back screen as house lights fade. Fade signature. LIGHTS ON BAND when house lights to B.O. NIGHT AND DAY—intro. followed by drum roll. Pin-spot s.c. floor-level on* SOLO MALE:)

WOULDN'T IT BE FUN?

Wouldn't it be fun not to be famous?
Wouldn't it be fun not to be rich?
Wouldn't it be pleasant
To be a simple peasant
And spend a happy day digging a ditch?
Wouldn't it be fun
Not to be known as an important VIP?
Wouldn't it be fun
To be nearly anyone
Except me, mighty me!

(*Same singer continues as* NARRATOR.)

NARRATOR. But Cole Porter <u>was</u> famous, he <u>was</u> rich, and he <u>was</u> a VIP, and he wrote songs in the days when writing musicals was still fun. All together, he wrote twenty six openings to twenty six shows . . .

(*Pin-spot fades on* SOLO MALE. *B.O., during which* BAND *plays* NIGHT AND DAY *intro seguing into intro to* ANOTHER OP'NIN', ANOTHER SHOW, *during which* COMPANY *enter. Five* GIRLS *on top level, five* BOYS *underneath floor-level. During the number,* PROJECTIONS *run through all the titles of CP shows ending in a montage of show-titles at end of number.*)

COMPANY. ANOTHER OP'NIN', ANOTHER SHOW

(*LIGHTS up on* GIRLS *top-level.*)

GIRLS.
Another op'nin', another show,
In Philly, Boston or Baltimo',

>   (*LIGHTS up on* BOYS *on floor-level.*)

BOYS.
A chance for stage-folks to say hello,
ALL.
Another op'nin', another show.
>   (GIRLS *begin to descend stairs,* BOYS *to break up group* S.C. *They form different couple-formations during the number.*)

Another job that you hope at last,
Will make your future forget your past,
Another pain where the ulcers grow,
Another op'nin' of another show.
MAN.
Four weeks!
ALL.
You rehearse and rehearse.
MAN.
Three weeks!
ALL.
And it couldn't be worse!
MAN.
One week!
ALL.
Will it ever be right?
Then out of the hat, it's that big first night!
>   (*LIGHTS have built up to general cover.* COMPANY *reprise the lyric as whisper-chorus:*)

Another op'nin, another show,
In Philly, Boston or Baltimo',
A chance for stage folks to say hello,
Another op'nin' of another show.
Another job that you hope at last
Will make your future forget your past,
Another pain where the ulcers grow,
Another op'nin' of another show.
Four weeks you rehearse and rehearse
Three weeks and it couldn't be worse,
One week will it ever be right,
Then out of the hat, it's that big first night!

The overture is about to start . . .
   (*TRUMPET break.*)
You cross your fingers and hold your heart.
   (*HEARTBEAT break.*)
It's curtain time and away we go,
Another op'nin' . . .
   (COMPANY *break up* S.C. *groups and begin to exit severally.*)
   COMPANY. (*Cont.*)
Just another op'nin',
Of—another—show!

(COMPANY *off except* TWO NARRATORS. NARRATOR ONE *to* D.S.L. *and* TWO *to half-level* S.R. *LIGHTS change to single spot on* NARRATOR ONE.)

NARRATOR 1. Cole Porter was one of Broadway's classic success-stories and spent most of his life in the international spotlight. Consequently, he was a much-photographed man . . . (*PROJECTIONS: Montage of sepia photographs of CP's international period.*) Cole Porter in Paris, Cole Porter in Venice, on the Riviera, in Rio, in London, in New York. The music and the life-style seem to typify an era when sophisticated glamour captured the popular imagination, but like so many success stories, Porter's began in a rather less glamorous, less sophisticated way, in the unlikely small mid-Western town of Peru, Indiana . . .

(*FADE spot on* NARRATOR 1, *who exits. Cross-fade to spot on* NARRATOR 2. *PROJECTIONS: Dissolve to sepia picture of Main Street, Peru at turn of century filling whole screen except for the sides. PIANO plays* BOBOLINK WALTZ *softly underneath this speech.*)

NARRATOR 2. . . . An unpaved Main Street called Broadway, a vaudeville theatre, a nickelodeon, a circus—once a year, a symphony concert—once a year, a father who read Robert Browning with the boy, a mother he adored (*PROJECTIONS: bring up picture of Kate Porter on* R. *of screen.*) and who had his precocious song-writing efforts privately published, and a dominating tycoon of a grandfather (*PROJECTIONS: bring up J.C. Cole on* L. *of screen.*). When he was thirteen, his parents with that characteristic gesture of the bourgeoisie, demonstrated their joy at having him around the place by sending him away from it. He was shipped East to

Worcester Academy . . . (*PROJECTIONS: Dissolve to sepia shot of CP at Worcester.*) Editor of the School Magazine, co-pianist of the Glee Club, leading man in the class play, president of the Mandolin Club. And then, in 1910, with his own piano amongst his luggage, Cole Porter arrived at Yale . . .

B) *YALE*

(*LIGHTS fade on* NARRATOR 2 *who exits. LIGHTS change to pool of light on top level* S.L. *into which enters* NARRATOR 3 *for following speech, which is from Gerald Murphy's Recollections of Cole Porter at Yale taken from Calvin Tompkins' "Living Well is the Best Revenge." PROJECTIONS dissolve to montage of Yale shots [still in sepia] in 1910.*)

NARRATOR 3. (*As* MURPHY.) There was this barbaric custom of going around to the rooms of the sophomores and talking with them, to see which ones would be the right material for the fraternities. I remember going around and seeing several nights running, a sign on one boy's door saying "Back at 10 pm. Gone to football-song practice." Some were enormously irritated that *anyone* would have the gall to be out of the room on visiting nights and determined not to call on him at all. But one night, I was passing his room and went in, just to say hello . . . (*PROJECTIONS: bring up shot of CP at piano in rooms at Yale.*) There was a single electric light bulb in the corner of the ceiling, wicker furniture, which was considered a bad sign at Yale in 1911, a piano with a box of caramels on it, and a little dark man with his hair parted in the middle and slicked back, wearing a salmon-pink tie and a checked suit, looking like a westerner dressed up for the east . . . He told me that he *had* submitted a song for the football team and that it had just been accepted . . .

(*Offstage whistle blown.* CHEERLEADER *runs on.*)

CHEER-L. Gimme a Y!
3 GIRLS. (*Offstage.*) Y!
CHEER-L. Gimme an A!
GIRLS. A!
CHEER-L. Gimme an L!
GIRLS. L!
CHEER-L. Gimme an E!
GIRLS. E!
CHEER-L. What have you got?

GIRLS. (*Running on with streamers in hands.*) YALE!!!
ALL. Y-A-L-E!

(*BAND go into* BINGO ELI YALE! *intro for* QUARTET:)

BINGO ELI YALE!

Bingo! Bingo!
Bingo, Bingo, Bingo that's the lingo!
Eli is bound to win.
There's to be a victory so watch the team begin!
Bingo! Bingo!
Harvard's team cannot prevail.
Fight! Fight!
Fight with all your might,
For Bingo, Bingo Eli Yale!

(*They run off cheering. LIGHTS fade back to Spot on* NARRATOR 3 *who continues as* MURPHY. *PROJECTIONS: Screen fades to black.*)

NARRATOR 3. . . . we had long talks about music and composers—we were both crazy about Gilbert and Sullivan. I got the Glee Club to take him on as a sophomore, something that was almost never done—and they introduced several new songs he had written . . .

(*LIGHTS fade on* NARRATOR *who sits on steps below top level* L. *PROJECTIONS: Superimpose moonlight scene over Yale picture. LIGHTS cross fade to pool on* BARBERSHOP QUARTET S.L. *They move across stage during song and LIGHTS build to cover accordingly.*)

WHEN THE SUMMER MOON COMES ' LONG

MALE QUARTET.
Verse 1

If you want to wed a little girl,
Simply wild about her,
Couldn't live without her,
If your heart's completely in a whirl,
Just want to love and spoon;

Don't propose while winter time is here,
Wait till stars are gleaming,
Winking, blinking, beaming,
Now's the time to ask your little dear,
Under the summer moon.

Refrain 1

First select a small canoe,
Where there's only room for two,
You'll love her and she'll love you,
You could never get in wrong,
While the stars are shining bright
In the silv'ry, dreamy night,
You can hold her, fold her tight,
When the summer moon comes 'long.

Verse 2

When you've popped the question to her too,
After you have kissed her
She'll only be your 'sister,'
Then declare that you're completely through,
Paddle her back home soon.
Drift along until you've met a queen,
Someone who will marry,
Won't put off or tarry,
Take her to the spot where you've just been
Under the summer moon.

Refrain 2

First select a small canoe,
Where there's only room for two,
You'll love her and she'll love you,
You could never get in wrong.
While the stars are shining bright
In the silv'ry dreamy night,
You can hold her, fold her tight . . .

(*They hold this last note. LIGHTS back on* NARRATOR 3 *who stands and begins to come down steps* S.L.)

NARRATOR 3. Porter at Yale worked very hard indeed. Member of the Dramatic Club and the Glee Club . . . (*He indicates* QUARTET *at opposite side stage.*)

QUARTET.
When the summer moon comes 'long.

(QUARTET *extend last note and* THREE *of them exit still humming last note which overlaps following lines. There should be no attempt to get applause after "Summer Moon." Fourth member remains on stage as* NARRATOR 4.)

NARRATOR 3. When he left Yale, Porter told people he expected to go into either mining, lumbering or farming.

NARRATOR 4. In fact he did not go into mining, he did not go into lumbering and he did not go into farming. What he did go into was Harvard. His grandfather, who controlled the cash flow, insisted that young Porter studied Law at Harvard. So there he went and graduated—in music.

NARRATOR 3. By now he was obsessed with the musical theatre to the exclusion of everything else and in 1916 he had completed a kind of comic opera, his first full Broadway score . . . (NARRATOR 4 *conducts BAND for fanfare intro. to "SEE AMERICA FIRST."*)
"See America First."

(*PROJECTIONS: Stars and stripes blow-up. First colour projection. LIGHTS fade on* NARRATORS. *Spot* S.C. *into which enters* SOLO FEMALE *for* SEE AMERICA FIRST. *Dressed in US flag, swift move on and straight into number:*)

SEE AMERICA FIRST

Don't leave America,
Just stick around the U.S.A.
Cheer for America
And get that grand old strain of Yankee Doodle
In your noodle.
Yell for America,
Altho' your vocal chords may burst;
And if you ever take an outing,
Leave the station shouting
"See America First"!

(*Closing fanfare coda during which* SINGER *exits* U.S.L. *and* S.L. *on* NARRATORS 3 *and* 4. NARRATOR 4 *takes a newspaper from top of piano and turns pages.*)

NARRATOR 4. (*Reading.*) "You would be well advised, in considering the latest musical offerings on Broadway, to see "See America First" last." (*He reads more.*) "The latest, the newest, the worst musical in town."
NARRATOR 3. (*Indicating* NARRATOR 4.) It was so bad that even the cast hated it.
NARRATOR 4. (*Folds paper and puts it under his arm.*) I played a Cowboy and an Autumn Flower. Others had roles not so believable.

(*He turns and exits* U.S.C. *LIGHTS fade to just spot on* NARRATOR 3 S.L.)

NARRATOR 3. It was the only Cole Porter show in history where the audience came out humming a Gershwin tune. "See America First" collapsed under its own weight after 15 performances and Porter retired in what he firmly believed was disgrace. The fact was that nobody even noticed it had closed. But his course of action was the classic one. Having advised audiences to see America first without taking the precaution of first seeing it for himself, he went where Oscar Wilde said all good Americans go. In the autumn of 1917 he was seen boarding the liner "Espagna" bound for the new Mecca for young Americans—Paris, France . . .

C) *PARIS*

(*LIGHTS fade on* NARRATOR *who exits* D.S.L. *LIGHTS to general cover. BAND plays upbeat chorus of "See America First" during which departure scene is staged. PURSER enters to* S.C. *with passenger list, ticking off passengers as they leave.* TWO FLAPPERS *excitedly coming down* S.R. *stairs from top level, a rich* LADY PASSENGER *from* U.S.C. *and a brash* MILLIONAIRE. *They mime checking with* PURSER *and all cross to steps* S.L. *as if embarking liner. Orchestral intro. segues into intro. to "Lost Liberty Blues" and* PASSENGERS *freeze. PROJECTIONS: Overlap departure scene with sequence of stills of Manhattan Harbour, throughout which Statue of Liberty emerges larger and larger until it is in centre of frame.* FEMALE SINGER *dressed in showgirl-Statue of Liberty costume enters on top level so she seems to emerge from the frame. Sings to departing tourists:*)

LOST LIBERTY BLUES

Verse

As you sail away
On your holiday,
Take a last little look at me . . .
    (*Departing* PASSENGERS *exeunt upstairs* S.L. *and off top level.*)
I'm an innocent
Public monument
Called the Statue of Liberty.
And I'm a slave in the land of the brave and the home of the free.
Once my country France
Had a Yank romance,
So they gave me to Uncle Sam.
But he's changed me so
I no longer know
What I'm meant for
Or who I am.
He's made a mess
Of my chance for success
And I'm not worth a damn.
    (*Music takes on bump-and-grind feeling.*)

Refrain

I've got the Lost Liberty Blues,
Those Lost Liberty Blues;
With a pair of handcuffs on my wrists
And padlocks on my shoes.
Can you expect me to be gay,
Or ask me to enthuse?
While Reformers lead 'em
To the Battle Cry of Freedom,
To the Lost Liberty Blues.
    (SINGER *comes down steps* S.L. *to half-level.*)
Adieu, Adieu Liberté perdue,
Vers vous mon ami perdue,
Tourne ses souvenirs et ses plus
Imperieux desirs.
Adieu, adieu mon liberté morte,
Au loin le vent vous emporte,
Touts fols espoir de mon coeur

Et desormais a tout jamais
Banni! Ah, tout est fini!
>   (*She turns and goes back up to top level for ending.*)

Can you expect me to be gay,
Or ask me to enthuse?
While Reformers lead 'em
To the Battle Cry of Freedom
To the Lost Liberty Blues.

>   (*Big blues finish on "Blues" at end of which she blows torch out and LIGHTS fade to B.O. PROJECTIONS: Statue and Stars and Stripes dissolve to French tricolour flag. LIGHTS: spot up on half-level* S.R. *into which* NARRATOR [*Male*] *enters.*)

NARRATOR. By the time Porter arrived in Paris, there were so many Americans living there that it had become the third largest city in the United States. The expatriates weren't too good about speaking French, however. Most of them were still having trouble enough with English. As you wandered through the cafes and night-clubs you might come across the occasional writer so decrepit he'd have to check the obituary columns each morning to make sure he wasn't there, or the occasional painter so schizophrenic that he'd have to get someone else to paint his self-portrait. But there were others, like Cole Porter, who had a deep and abiding affection for Paris . . .

>   (*During last lines of the preceding speech,* SOLO FEMALE *singer enters to top level* [LADY PASSENGER *from departure scene*] *She stands, back to audience in silhouette looking at PROJECTIONS which have dissolved to whole-screen image of an Impressionist painting of Paris* [*suggest Pissarro oil of Paris bridges*] *As spot fades on* NARRATOR *who exits, LIGHTS come up on top level and she turns and begins to sing:*)

I LOVE PARIS

Verse

Ev'ry time I look down
On this timeless town,
Whether grey or blue be her skies,
Whether loud be her cheers

Or whether soft be her tears,
More and more do I realize . . .
   (*She comes down steps* S.L. *bottom rostrum.*)

Refrain

I love Paris in the springtime,
I love Paris in the fall,
I love Paris in the winter when it drizzles,
I love Paris in the summer when it sizzles,
I love Paris ev'ry moment,
Ev'ry moment of the year,
I love Paris,
Why, oh why do I love Paris?
Because my love is near.
   (*She comes to centre stage for reprise half-chorus.*)
I love Paris ev'ry moment,
Ev'ry moment of the year,
I love Paris,
Why, oh why do I love Paris?
Because my love is near . . .

(*BAND segue directly into intro. to "Do You Want to See Paris?" No applause-break after "I Love Paris"* FRENCH GUIDE *enters, also the* TWO FLAPPERS *and the* MILLIONAIRE. GUIDE *runs up to "I Love Paris" singer. PROJECTIONS: Dissolve to Dufy painting of map of Paris.*)

   GUIDE.
Do you want to see Paris?
   (SINGER *shakes her head and exits* U.S.C. *He turns to others.*)
Do you want to see Paris?
If you want to see Paris,
Then come along with me.
   FLAPPERS.
We want to see Paris,
We want to see Paris.
   MILLIONAIRE.
And see how Paris
Compares with Kankakee.
   GUIDE.
Then why not join my guided tour?

FLAPPERS.
First how much is it sonny?
GUIDE.
It's only fifty francs apiece.
MILLIONAIRE.
What's that in American money?
GUIDE.
Well, fifty francs divided by three
And multiplied by seven
Makes let me see, let me see . . .
MILLIONAIRE.
Why you damn fool, eleven.
FLAPPERS.
Is that all? Is that all?
He's talking through his hat.
MILLIONAIRE.
You couldn't get a ride in a baby-carriage
In the USA for that.

(They all fall in for tour.)

GUIDE.
We are now going up the Champs Elysees, if you please,
You see those poles sticking out of the ground,
Those are trees.
FLAPPERS.
Poor little trees,
They've got some strange disease.
GUIDE.
That building there, upon the right
Is the famous Hotel Claridge.
It's where the ladies go at night
When they get fed up with marriage.
FLAPPERS.
Hurrah for the Claridge!
And down with marriage!
GUIDE.
And now before you, straight ahead, the Arc de Triomphe stands
To commemorate the victories of France in many lands.
It was built in eighteen hundred and five
By Napoleon the Great.
FLAPPERS.
'Swonderful! 'Smarvellous! It'd make such a nice front gate.

GUIDE.
It's a hundred and sixty four feet high,
And a hundred and fifty wide,
And exactly seventy two feet deep.
 FLAPPERS.
Well, say you're some Guide!
 GUIDE.
This great Arcade
Stands all alone,
But unafraid
Upon her throne,
Entirely made
Of solid stone.
 MILLIONAIRE.
I'll buy it!

(PROJECTIONS: Fade to Eiffel Tower outline screen-centre.)

 GUIDE.
Before you stands the Eiffel Tower
A monument adored.
 MILLIONAIRE.
Then what's that sign mean "Citroen"?
 GUIDE.
"Citroen" is French for "Ford."
 FLAPPERS.
Aux armes, citoyens,
Citroen is French for Ford.

(Tour now moves all over various levels of the set. Up steps S.L. *to top level.)*

 GUIDE.
Do you realise this famous tow'r
Will be all lit up in another hour
By the light of a million candle pow'r?
 MILLIONAIRE.
I'll buy it!

(PROJECTIONS: Dissolve to Madeleine outline.)

 GUIDE.
Kneel in pray'r

And doff your hat,
And cease your remarks profane,
The building there
You're gazing at,
Is the famous Church of the Madeleine.
    FLAPPERS.
Hallelujah! Hallelujah!
For the Madeleine!
    MILLIONAIRE.
We've got a Church in Kankakee,
But this one is a riot,
So if you'll send it C.O.D.,
I'll buy it!

(*PROJECTIONS: Dissolve to Moulin Rouge sign.* GUIDE *leads them down steps* S.R. *as BAND goes into Can-Can break. Gartered leg doing can-can movements appears from one of the* U.S.C. *entrances.*)

    GUIDE.
We are now in the Moulin Rouge,
An old Parisian pet,
Where the men that girls remember
Meet the girls that men forget.
Its promenade is an ideal spot
For a man whose French is not so hot
To improve his French with a French cocotte.

(MILLIONAIRE *spots leg and catches it in mid-movement and exits following it.*)

    MILLIONAIRE.
I'll buy it!

(FLAPPERS *come in* D.S.C. *with* GUIDE *between them.*)

    GUIDE.
Goodnight, everybody.
    FLAPPERS.
Good evening, Mister Guide.
We're glad that we've seen Paris,
And thanks for the lovely ride.

(FLAPPERS *begin to leave.*)

GUIDE.
But please, before you leave me
And go back to your huts,
Will you kindly tell me what you think of Paris?
FLAPPERS.
It's for nuts!

(FLAPPERS *go off* D.S.L. GUIDE *left alone as lights fade.* NARRATOR *entering slowly to half-level* S.R. *as PROJECTIONS fade to black.*)

GUIDE.
Do you want to see Paris?
Do you want to see Paris?
(*He goes* U.S. *to below* NARRATOR *and looks up at him.*)
Do you want to see Paris?
(NARRATOR *shakes his head.* GUIDE *turns to exit* U.S.C. *as lights fade to spot only on* NARRATOR.)
I thank you.

(NARRATOR *turns to audience.*)

NARRATOR. This was the period that set the lasting image—the beachrobed socialite basking in the noonday sun in the fashionable resorts of the international set whose heyday was the long cocktail party that was the 1920's. Cole Porter became one of the first men to race a speedboat on the canals of Venice . . . (*PROJECTIONS: Slowly fade up montage of CP in 1920's—Venice Lido etc.*) and a pioneer American coloniser of the Riviera. There were parties in Paris, parties in Antibes, costume balls in his palazzo in Venice; Elsa Maxwell played hostess and Noël Coward, Fanny Brice and the Diaghilev Ballet provided the cabaret. The places changed but the faces remained the same, moving from the terrace, the beach, the yacht, the Society columns and the guest lists . . .

(*Intro to "Mrs Lowsborough Goodby" played softly underneath last part of this speech, during which LIGHTS come up slowly and* BELLBOY *enters from* U.S.C. *crossing stage with suitcase to exit* S.L. *He is followed by* RICH AMERICAN SOCIALITE *in expensive fur-trimmed coat, who slowly comes to* S.C. *and then as*

LIGHTS *come up to full level at end of* NARRATOR'*s speech, comes right* D.S. *to audience.* PROJECTIONS: *Dissolve to full-screen image of luxury Hotel foyer.* [*Suggest painting of Dorchester foyer as reproduced in Harold Arlen's "A Young Man Comes to London"*] *Spot on* NARRATOR *out leaving female singer alone for "Mrs Lowsborough."*)

MRS LOWSBOROUGH-GOODBY

Verse

Mrs Lowsborough-Goodby gives weekends,
And her weekends are not a success,
But she asks you so often,
You finally soften
And end by answering "Yes."
When I left Mrs Lowsborough-Goodby's.
The letter I wrote was polite,
But it would have been bliss
Had I dared write her this,
The letter I wanted to write . . .

Refrain

Thank you so much Mrs. Lowsborough-Goodby,
    Thank you so much
Thank you so much for that infinite weekend with you.
Thank you a lot Mrs. Lowsborough-Goodby, thank you a lot.
And don't be surprised if you suddenly should be
Quietly shot.
For the clinging perfume
Of that damp little room,
For those cocktails so hot,
And the bath that was not,
For those guests so amusing and mentally bracing
Who talked about racing and racing—and racing.
For the ptomaine I got from your famous Pink Salmon.
For the fortune I lost when you taught me backgammon,
For those mornings I passed with your dear, but deaf mother,
For those evenings I spent with that bounder your brother,
And for making me swear to myself there and then
Never to go for a weekend again,

Thank you so much Mrs Lowsborough-Goodby
(*Note*: this time pronounced Louse-borough)
Thank you—
Thank you—sooooo much!

(SINGER *exits* D.S.L. *LIGHTS back on* NARRATOR *in spot half-level* S.R. *PROJECTIONS: Fade to black.*)

NARRATOR. He deliberately fostered the impression of elegant idler, a sort of musical Court Jester to the international set. But he said later that he could remember almost nothing of this period because his mind was focused elsewhere. He kept up a front of blithe indifference to the lack of offers from Broadway or London and pretended that he wrote songs only to amuse himself and his friends. At any rate, in 1923 his old Yale friend Gerald Murphy came to his rescue . . . (*PROJECTIONS: Small projection of Murphy's original parody-tabloid backcloth for "Within the Quota."*) Both had by now made the inevitable expatriate's discovery; the further you drift from home, the closer the outlines of home become. To Murphy's designs and libretto, he composed a jazz-ballet, "Within the Quota," a kind of satirical projection of American archetypes—the Cowboy, the World's Sweetheart and . . . the Jazz Baby . . .

(*LIGHTS cross-fade to pin-spot on* DANCER *for Ballet-Extract, in black sequined tunic, face hidden behind large feathered fan.* NARRATOR *exits. As first piano chords of the Ballet begin,* DANCER *begins to take fan away from face and come* D.S. *for the number. LIGHTS change to colour-wheel lights over* S.C. *PROJECTIONS: Cross-fade small tabloid image to full-scale one filling the entire screen. BALLET: "Jazz Baby" sequence from "Within the Quota." The ballet extract should be cut if a reduced company has not the choreographic resources for this number. As extract ends,* DANCER *turns with back to audience with fan held behind her and begins to go* U.S.C. *BAND: Direct segue into intro. to "Dizzy Baby." During this,* TWO MALE DANCERS *enter [One is* NARRATOR *from last speech who comes to half-level* S.R. *and the other comes on from top level entrance to the opposite half-level]. LIGHTS build to more general cover as they begin to sing and dance "Dizzy Baby" to her. No PROJECTIONS change.*)

DIZZY BABY

FIRST MALE.
Sweet Baby you're a saint.
I've only one complaint—
You go so fast
I can't keep up with you.

(*He jumps off* S.L. *half-level as the other begins to sing coming down steps* S.R.)

2ND MALE.
I'm tired of op'ning plays,
And closing matinees,
I'd rather breakfast, dear, than sup with you.
 BOTH.
Why don't you let me make a bride of you,
And stop that dynamo inside of you?

Refrain

Dizzy Baby,
Dizzy Baby,
Won't you please slow down?
Can't you find one moment to relax?
Look behind—I'm falling in your tracks.
You're so busy
Being dizzy,
I get dizzy too—
Still, it may be
Because you're dizzy baby,
I love you.
 (*DANCE BREAK—Dixieland chorus, into reprised half-chorus.*)
You're so busy,
Being dizzy,
I get dizzy too—
Still, it may be
Because you're dizzy baby,
I love you.

(*One* MAN *carries* DANCER *off on his shoulders, leaving other holding fan. Quick take and blackout. LIGHTS: pool on steps just below half-level* S.L. *into which* FEMALE NARRATOR *enters.*)

NARRATOR. Several times during the '20's, Porter slipped back into New York in sporadic attempts to make good on Broadway. By now, of course, he was being asked the age-old question—"Which comes first, Mr Porter? The words or the music?" To which he always gave the perfectly honest answer—"Yes." But nobody in Broadway's producing offices took much notice of one they regarded as an international playboy composer until 1928 when he wrote a show that marked the end of a phase in his life. Having begun the decade by not taking his own advice to see America first, he ended it with a musical celebration of his own retreat to Europe. Sensing that the time had come for a once-and-for-all bid for Broadway, he made that bid with a show called "Paris" . . .

(*LIGHTS change to more general cover.* PURSER *appears from* U.S.C. *and comes to* S.C. *The* NARRATOR *is the first to go to him to check as* DEPARTING PASSENGER, *followed by the* MILLIONAIRE, *then the "Mrs. Lowsborough" single, one of the "Dizzy Baby" boys and, finally, one of the* FLAPPERS. *This departure is staged more slowly than the earlier one from New York to Paris. They all cross to* S.R. *slowly and group themselves on* S.R. *steps. As they cross,* GUIDE *from "Do You Want to See Paris?" appears on top-level looking down on them and begins "You Don't Know Paree." PROJECTIONS: Superimpose faint Dufy painting behind Murphy tabloid.*)

YOU DON'T KNOW PAREE

You come to Paris,
You come to play,
You have a wonderful time,
You go away,
And from then on you talk of Paris knowingly,
You may know Paris, you don't know Paree.

Though you've been around a lot,
And danced a lot and laughed a lot,
You don't know Paree.
You may say you've seen a lot
And heard a lot
And learned a lot,
You don't know Paree.
Paree will still be laughing after

Ev'ry one of us disappears,
But never once forget her laughter
Is the laughter that hides the tears,
And until you've lived a lot
And loved a lot
And lost a lot,
You don't know Paree,
You don't know Paree . . .

> (SINGER *comes down to half-level* S.L. *Groups* S.R. *still in half-light.* PROJECTIONS: *Very slowly begin to lose superimposed Dufy leaving the tabloid on its own by end of number.*)

Paree will still be laughing after
Ev'ry one of us disappears,
But never once forget her laughter
Is the laughter that hides the tears.
And until you've lived a lot,
And loved a lot,
And lost a lot,
You won't know Paree,
You won't know—Paree . . .

(BAND *segue into intro. to "Take Me Back to Manhattan."* SINGER *exits* D.S.L. LIGHTS: *Bring up lights* S.R. *on group on steps.* PROJECTIONS: *Couples sequence. At start of "Take Me Back To Manhattan," fade tabloid backcloth except for single skyscraper* R. *on screen. During the number, gradually repeat the skyscraper image until it is repeated right across screen. Then, just before end of number, superimpose behind the master-slide of abstract shapes for the New York sequence.*)

D) MANHATTAN

TAKE ME BACK TO MANHATTAN

Verse

MILLIONAIRE.
The more I travel
Across the gravel,
  PURSER.
The more I sail the sea,
  MRS L-G SINGER.
The more I feel convinced of the fact,

New York's the place for me.
> MALE.

Its crazy skyline
Is right in my line,
> FEMALE.

And when I'm far away,
> TOURIST.

I'm able to bear it for several hours,
> FLAPPER.

And then I break down and say . . .

Refrain

> ALL. (*Still seated.*)

Take me back to Manhattan,
Take me back to New York,
I'm just longing to see once more
My little room on the hundredth floor.
Can you wonder I'm gloomy?
Can you smile when I frown?
I miss the East Side, the West Side,
The North Side, and the South Side, so
Take me back to Manhattan,
That dear old dirty town.

> (*SOUND: Ship's hooter.* TOURISTS *all stand and begin to go upstairs* S.R. *on to half-level and top-level as if disembarking.*)

I miss the East Side, the West Side,
The North Side and the South Side, so
Take me back to Manhattan,
I wanna go back,
Yes I wanna go back,
So take me back to Manhattan,
To that dear—old—dirty—town!

(*They exit through various entrances. As they go,* SOLO MALE *comes on from* S.R. *half-level entrance up to top-level centre in to spot against skyline shot for next passage of narration [from F. Scott Fitzgerald "My Lost City"] and following number.*)

> NARRATOR. As the ship glided up the river, the city burst thunderously upon us in the early dusk—the white glacier of lower New York swooping down like the strand of a bridge to rise into uptown

New York, a miracle of foamy light suspended by stars. A band started to play on deck but the majesty of the city made the march trivial and tinkling. From that moment, I knew that New York, however often I might leave it, was home . . .

(*Intro to "I Happen to Like New York" has begun under last lines of this speech.* SINGER *goes straight into it from the speech. Still in spot top-level centre.*)

I HAPPEN TO LIKE NEW YORK

I happen to like New York,
I happen to like this town,
I like the city air, I like to drink of it,
The more I know New York the more I think of it,
I like the sight and sound and even the stink of it,
I happen to like New York;
I like to go to Battery Park,
And watch those liners booming in,
I often ask myself why should it be,
That they should come so far across the sea,
I suppose it's because they all agree with me,
They happen to like New York.
   (SINGER *moves across top-level and comes down* S.R. *steps to stage-level* C. *LIGHTS: build to general cover.*)
Last Sunday afternoon,
I took a trip to Hackensack,
But after I gave Hackensack the once-over
I took the next train back.
I happen to like New York,
I happen to love this burgh,
And when I have to give the world a last farewell,
And the undertaker starts to ring my funeral bell,
I don't want to go to heaven, don't want to go to hell.
   (COMPANY *coming on, to various levels all over stage, to join in last lines.*)
I happen to like—I happen to like—
I happen to like—New York!

(*BAND: Direct segue into intro. to "Big Town."* COMPANY *begin in it positions spread out over whole stage.*)

BIG TOWN

Big Town,
What's before me?
Fair weather or stormy?
Big Town, will I hit the heights
And see my name in electric lights?

> (COMPANY *all begin coming down from various levels to floor level, ending in group* U.S.C. *backs to audience, arms up looking at skyline in screen. Except for the "I Happen to Like New York"* NARRATOR/SINGER *who keeps apart and goes to* D.S.L. *rostrum.*)

Big town will I blunder,
Fall down or go under,
Or will I rise and rise
Till I scrape your skies?
Big town,
Wise old town,
What's the low-down on me?

> (*LIGHTS: Change to backlight on* U.S. *group so they are in silhouette.* GIRL *and* BOY *for "52nd Street" slip off* U.S. [*for change costume—others begin N.Y. sequence in their costumes for the whole sequence*] *Spot on* NARRATOR D.S.L. *During the next speech,* COMPANY *in stylised attitudes, break the pose from end of "Big Town" and take on frozen Nightclub poses. LIGHTS change to smoky red back-light. PROJECTIONS: Superimpose red "Bar" and "Club" signs on screen behind master-slide.*)

NARRATOR. (*Wheeling round and cutting right into end of "Big Town."*) The tempo of the city had changed sharply. The uncertainties of 1920 were drowned in a steady golden roar and many of our friends had grown wealthy. But the restlessness of New York now approached hysteria; the pace was faster, the catering to dissipation set an example to Paris, the shows were broader, the buildings were higher, the morals were looser and the liquor was cheaper, but all these benefits did not minister to much delight. Young people wore out early—they were hard and languid at twenty-one. Many people who were not alcoholics were lit up four days out of seven and frayed nerves were strewn everywhere. Groups were held together by a generic nervousness and the hangover became a part of the day as well-allowed for as the Spanish siesta . . .

([*From F. Scott Fitzgerald, "My Lost City."*] *LIGHTS: Fade spot on* NARRATOR *who joins Nightclub group and finds a partner. During last part of speech, build lights half-level* S.R. *into which* SOLO MALE SINGER *for "I'm a Gigolo" enters. He looks down on people below, lights cigarette.* BAND *begins intro. to "Gigolo" during last words of speech and* SINGER *begins to descend steps.*)

I'M A GIGOLO

Verse

I should like you all to know
I'm a famous gigolo,
And of lavender, my nature's got just a dash in it.
As I'm slightly undersexed, you will always find me next
To some dowager who's wealthy rather than passionate.
Go to one of those nightclub places
And you'll find me stretching my braces
Pushing ladies with lifted faces
Round the floor.
But I must confess to you
There are moments when I'm blue
And I ask myself whatever I do it for . . .

(*ORCHESTRAL BREAK: Couples alter positions.* GIGOLO *on floor-level. He crosses front of stage during chorus to end in spot* D.S.L. *rostrum.*)

Refrain

I'm a flower who blooms in the winter
Sinking deeper and deeper in "snow,"
I'm a baby who has
No mother but jazz,
I'm a gigolo.
Ev'ry morning, when labour is over
To my sweet-scented lodgings I go,
Take a glass from the shelf
And look at myself—
I'm a gigolo.

I get stocks and bonds
From faded blondes
Ev'ry twenty-fifth of December;
Still, I'm just a pet
That men forget
And only tailors remember.
>(LADIES *of the couples arrogantly beckon men to follow them as they go, in movements timed to "Gigolo" rhythm, to* U.S.C. *again. The* SOLO GIRL *who will perform "Love for Sale" later, appears under top-level* U.S.C. *too.*)

Yet when I see the way all the ladies
Treat their husbands who put up the dough,
You cannot think me odd
If then I thank God
I'm a gigolo.

(*He blows smoke from a cigarette into spotlight as he turns and exits* D.S.L. *PROJECTIONS: Change colour to cold, taking out the reds. LIGHTS: take out colour, building to more general cover. Early morning light.* COUPLES *still grouped* U.S. NEWSBOY *enters to half-level* S.L.)

NEWSBOY. (*Selling papers to couples who come* D.S. *to him and then exit severally by various exits.*)
Morning papers, morning papers,
Gang chief killed when explosion occurs,
Six months' bride says child isn't hers,
Admiral Byrd's bought a new set of furs,
Morning Papers,
Morning papers,
Morning papers,
Morning papers,
Well known clubman is put in the pen,
Clara Bow seen with several men,
Aimee MacPherson slugs her mother—again.
Morning papers, morning papers, morning papers, morning papers . . .

(COUPLES *all off. As* NEWSBOY's *voice fades away as he exits* D.S.R. *LIGHTS change to* SOLO FEMALE SINGER *in shaft of back-light* U.S.C. *beneath top-level.*)

LOVE FOR SALE

Verse

When the only sound in the empty street
Is the heavy tread of the heavy feet
That belong to the lonesome cop,
I open shop.
When the moon so long has been gazing down
On the wayward ways of this wayward town,
That her smile becomes a smirk,
I go to work . . .
    (*LIGHTS build to more general cover* S.C. *as she comes forward.*)

Refrain

Love for sale,
Appetizing young love for sale,
Love's that fresh and still unspoiled,
Love that's only slightly soiled,
Love for sale.
Who will buy?
Who would like to sample my supply?
Who's prepared to pay the price
For a trip to Paradise?
Love for sale.
Let the poets pipe of love
In their childish way.
I know ev'ry type of love
Better far than they.
If you want the thrill of love,
I've been through the mill of love,
Old love, new love,
Ev'ry love but true love,
Love for sale . . .
    (*She moves over to steps* S.L. *and as she does, LIGHTS change to spot beside* U.S.L. *half-level exit into which she moves.*)
Appetizing young love for sale.
If you want to buy my wares,
Follow me and climb the stairs,
Love for sale,
Love for sale . . .

(*She exits off half-level* L. *holding extended last note. As she leaves,* FEMALE NARRATOR *appears from* R. *to centre top-level looking after her. Then turns to audience. PROJECTIONS: Change to collage of Manhattan night skyline.*)

NARRATOR. The city fluctuated in muffled roars like the dim applause rising to an actor on the stage of a vast theatre. The shopgirls were looking like Marilyn Miller. Moving picture actresses were famous. Paul Whiteman played the significance of amusement on his violin. They were having the breadline at the Ritz that year. Everybody was there. People met people they knew in hotel lobbies smelling of orchids and plush and detective stories. People were tired of the proletariat—everybody was famous. There wasn't much interest in private lives . . .

([*From Zelda Fitzgerald, "Save Me the Waltz."*] *BAND: segue into intro. to "When Love Beckoned on 52nd Street." LIGHTS fade to silhouette on* NARRATOR *who moves across top-level to* S.L. *Bring up floor-level LIGHTS* S.C. *PROJECTIONS change to Manhattan by day. Leaves, sunshine etc. Enter* YOUNG GIRL, *running on from* U.S.C. *to* D.S. *to audience.*)

WHEN LOVE BECKONED

Verse

I don't mean to cause a shock in the house,
But I'd like to know is there a doc' in the house,
Who will give first aid
To the most confused maid
In town?
I had oh, such sweet suburban ideas,
You know what I mean, Deanna Durbin ideas,
Till one fatal night, when somebody suddenly spoke . . .

(*Enter* BOYFRIEND *half-level* S.L.)

BOYFRIEND. Hi!
SHE. Hi!
 . . . And broke them all down.
(*She turns to audience again.*)

Refrain

I used to dream of a starlighted stream,
Where my man and I would first meet,
So try to surmise
My terrific surprise
When love beckoned,
In fifty-second street.

(*Brief DANCE BREAK, during which they dance away from each other.*)

He.
I thought a breeze would appear in the trees
And sing something tender and sweet,
But how could it sing
With a band playing swing,
When love beckoned
In fifty-second street?
Both. (*Coming together again.*)
Now when we want to coo
Country lanes are taboo,
And old west fifty-two
Is our favourite beat
(When we're on our feet).
So you can bet
We shall never forget
That mad second
When we first reckoned
That love beckoned
In fifty-second street.

(*Clinch at end and then they run off* U.S.C. *Fade LIGHTS* S.C. *and come back on top-level* C. *into which previous* Female Narrator *slowly moves. Also LIGHTS on half-level* S.R. *PROJECTIONS: Change to night Manhattan scene. Shapes of sky-scrapers outlined in lights.* Other Female Narrator *enters into* S.R. *half-level lights.*)

Narrator. Paul Whiteman played "Two Little Girls in Blue" at the Palais Royal. It was a big, expensive number. Girls with piquant profiles were mistaken for Gloria Swanson. New York was more full of reflections than of itself—the only concrete things in town were the abstractions. Everyone wanted to pay the cabaret checks. All over New York people telephoned. They telephoned from one hotel to another to people on other parties that they couldn't get there—that they were engaged. It was always teatime, or late at night . . .

(*[From "Save Me The Waltz."]* NARRATOR *moves during speech to* S.C. *and exits* U.S.C. *glancing up to top-level where previous* NARRATOR *has come into spot* C. *on level. She has been dressed in a black sequined gown from start of sequence. She holds a glass in her hand. In profile to the audience, she turns as* BAND *plays intro. to "Down in the Depths."*)

DOWN IN THE DEPTHS

Verse

Manhattan—I'm up a tree,
The one I've most adored
Is bored with me.
Manhattan—I'm awfully nice,
Nice people dine with me,
And even twice.
Yet the only one in the world I'm mad about
Talks of somebody else—
And walks out.
   (*She moves along top-level* L. *and comes down steps to half-level* L. *Fade top-level spot and lights up on half-level.*)

Refrain

With a million neon rainbows burning below me,
And a million blazing taxis raising a roar,
Here I sit, above the town
In my pet pailleted gown,
Down in the depths
On the ninetieth floor.
While the crowds in all the nightclubs punish the parquet,
And the bars are packed with couples calling for more,
I'm deserted and depressed,
In my regal eagle nest,
Down in the depths
On the ninetieth floor.

When the only one you wanted wants another,
What's the use of swank and cash in the bank galore?
Why, even my analyst's wife
Has a perfectly good love life,
And here am I,
Facing tomorrow,
Alone with my sorrow,
Down in the depths
On the ninetieth floor.

(*She toasts the backcloth of the city as she holds defiant last note. Fade LIGHTS as she exits off half-level* S.L. *Immediate crossfade to LIGHTS on half-level* R. *PROJECTIONS: Superimpose "Burlesque" flashing sign over skyscrapers.* MALE SINGER *comes into light half-level* R.)

COME ON IN

MAN.
Down in forty-second street,
Where fun is fun and heat is heat,
There's a barker man I know,
Who barks for a burlesque show.
   (*Enter* BARKER [*straw hat and shirt-sleeves*] *from* U.S.C. *He pulls out catwalk-piece from under half-level* S.L. *and then comes down to audience.*)
When he starts to sell his wares
As eight o'clock arrives,
Lovers leave their love affairs
And husbands chuck their wives
To hear him hollering once again . . .

(MAN *comes down to floor-level* S.R. *as* BARKER *comes* D.S.C. *to bark for the show both to audience and to* MAN.)

BARKER.
Gentlemen,
Gentlemen,
Pardon me if I call you gentlemen,
COME ON IN and see the show tonight,
Our girls are dynamite,
They'll raise your Fahrenheit,

COME ON IN and see the show,
COME ON IN and see our chicken farm,
Each chick's so full of charm,
She'll ring your fire alarm,
COME ON IN and see the show . . .

    (BURLESQUE MADAM *appears* D.S.L.)

MADAM.
There's a slant-eyed doll
Called Tokyo Moll . . .
 (SHOWGIRL *in Japanese kimono enters to half-level and then along catwalk.*)
She was last year's Miss Japan,
And when her hips
Do Nipponese nips,
Can she wave her fan?
Yes, she can.
 BARKER and MADAM.
COME ON IN and give the girls a glance
And if you take a chance,
They'll show you when they dance,
They've all been made in France.
 (*They urge on* MAN.)
COME ON IN
COME ON IN
COME ON IN and see the show!

  (*Another* SHOWGIRL *appears to bump and grind on catwalk.*)

MADAM.
There's a Southern find,
Who does a slow grind
That'll break you right in two.
 (SHOWGIRL *gets stuck doing splits on catwalk.*)
She keeps it clean
If you know what I mean,
But when she's all through,
So are you!

    (BARKER *helps girl up.*)

Barker and Madam and Girls.
COME ON IN and give the girls a glance,
And if you take a chance,
They'll show you when they dance,
They went to school in France,
COME ON IN,
COME ON IN,
COME ON IN and see the show!

(Barker *and* Madam *push* Man *over to catwalk.* Girls *pull him up so he sits on it with them above him dancing. DANCE BREAK: Hot dance for* Girls *along catwalk, ending with girl either side of* Man *so his head is trapped between their laps.*)

Girl 1.
If you go for apples, boss,
Why don't you try my apple sauce?
Girl 2.
If you go for pie, sweetheart,
Why don't you try my cherry tart?
Both.
If you go for candy, Judge,
Why don't you try my home-made fudge?

(Man *jumps off catwalk.* Girls *motioned off by* Madam *who urges* Man *inside.* Barker *pushes catwalk-piece back in.*)

Barker and Madam and Girls.
COME ON IN and view our chicken farm,
Each chick's so full of charm,
She'll ring your fire alarm,
COME ON IN,
COME ON IN,
COME ON IN and see the show!

(*As they exit, LIGHTS change to spot half-level* s.r. *PROJECTIONS: Change to black.* Female Narrator *comes in to spot.*)

Narrator. Even as he wrote down those rhythms and lyrics, Porter knew that the world they represented had gone forever. Indeed, that was why he wrote them down; it was a kind of sentimental doffing of the hat to the old days. Broadway in the early 1930's, pushed by the new talking pictures, was trying for something a little more sophisticated. And in 1932, with a show called "Gay Divorce," it got what it was looking for . . .

(*Fade spot* S.R. *and bring up bluish pool of light surrounding half-level and steps below* S.L. MALE SINGER *in tails enters into it.*)

E) BROADWAY

NIGHT AND DAY

MAN.
Like the beat beat beat of the tom-tom when the jungle shadows fall,
Like the tick tick tock of the stately clock as it stands against the wall,
Like the drip drip drip of the raindrops when a summer show'r is through,
So a voice within me keeps repeating—you, you, you.
 (GIRL DANCER *has appeared in silhouette on top-level.* LIGHTS: *Moving cloud-shapes on screen. Moonlight. She gradually dances down steps* S.R. *to floor-level, to which* MAN *also moves and joins him at end of first chorus.*)
Night and day, you are the one,
Only you beneath the moon and under the sun,
Whether near to me or far,
It's no matter, darling, where you are,
I think of you night and day.
Day and night, why is it so,
That this longing for you follows wherever I go?
In the roaring traffic's boom,
In the silence of my lonely room,
I think of you night and day.
Night and day under the hide of me,
There's an oh, such a hungry yearning burning inside of me,
And its torment won't be through
Till you let me spend my life making love to you
Day and night, night and day.
 (DANCE CHORUS. *At end of dance, girl spins away from her partner and begins to go up steps* S.L. *He sings after her as she goes, crossing to end up rostrum* S.L. *in spot as* LIGHTS *fade on rest of stage.*)

Night and day under the hide of me
There's an, oh such a hungry yearning burning inside of me
And its torment won't be through
Till you let me spend my life making love to you
Day and night, night and day.

(SHE *has crossed top-level and disappears through exit half-level* S.R. *as he stretches out arm to her as she disappears. Fade spot and clouds.* MAN *exits* D.S.L. *in blackout. Screen to black too.* LIGHTS *up in pool* D.S.R. *revealing* MALE NARRATOR *who has entered in blackout.* PROJECTIONS: *Bring in "Vanity Fair" cover of Jazz Age party.*)

NARRATOR. It was an age of miracles, it was an age of art, it was an age of excess and it was an age of satire. We were the most powerful nation. Who could tell us any longer what was fashionable and what was fun? . . . The Jazz Age was in flower. Scarcely had the staider citizens of the Republic caught their breaths when the wildest of all generations, the generation which had been adolescent during the confusion of the War, danced into the limelight. The sequel was like a children's party taken over by the elders, leaving the children puzzled and rather neglected and rather taken aback. The younger generation was starred no longer . . .

([*From F. Scott Fitzgerald "Echoes of the Jazz Age."*] *During the end of speech,* LIGHTS *up on half-level* S.L. *into which enters* FEMALE SINGER. *Rhythm section of* BAND *begin into. to "Anything Goes" at same time and she begins song cutting straight into end of narration, addressing* NARRATOR:)

ANYTHING GOES

SINGER.
Times have changed
And we've often rewound the clock
Since the Puritans got a shock
When they landed on Plymouth Rock . . .
    (COMPANY [*except two*] *enter in time to music.*)
If today,
Any shock they should try to stem,
'Stead of landing on Plymouth Rock,
Plymouth Rock would land on them.

COMPANY.
In olden days a glimpse of stocking
Was looked on as something shocking,
Now, heaven knows,
Anything goes.
  BOYS.
Good authors too, who once knew better words
Now only use four-letter words
Writing prose—
Anything goes.
  GIRLS.
If driving fast cars you like,
If low bars you like,
If old hymns you like,
If bare limbs you like,
If Mae West you like,
Or me undressed you like,
Why nobody will oppose.
  COMPANY.
When ev'ry night the set that's smart is
Intruding in nudist parties
In studios,
Anything goes.
    (*DANCE BREAK*. COUPLE *enter from* U.S. *for Tap-Charleston. Followed by Company tap-routine, then Solo drunk-tap sequence, seguing into second chorus*.)
When Grandmamma, whose age is eighty
In nightclubs is getting matey
With gigolos,
Anything goes.
The world has gone mad today,
And good's bad today,
And day's night today.
And black's white today,
  GIRLS.
And most guys today that women prize today
Are just silly gigolos.
  BOYS.
And though I'm not a great romancer,
I know that you're bound to answer when I propose,
  GIRLS.
Anything goes!

COMPANY.
Anything—anything—anything—
Anything goes!

(*Play-off music after applause for* COMPANY *exit, except for* OLDER MALE NARRATOR *who comes forward into spot* D.S.C. *PRO-JECTIONS: Dissolve to poster of "Anything Goes" with "Book by P.G. Wodehouse and Guy Bolton" clearly visible.*)

NARRATOR. One of Porter's collaborators on ANYTHING GOES was P. G. Wodehouse, who had one favourite recollection of how the show was put together. Wodehouse, Porter and Guy Bolton were scattered far afield, Wodehouse at his villa at Le Touquet, Bolton in Sussex, England, and Porter in Heidelberg. It was the director, Howard Lindsay, who suggested that the three men might find it easier to work together if they met occasionally.

Finally, the team gathered at Le Touquet, and naturally the first thing that Bolton and Wodehouse wanted to do was to hear the music Porter had written and so, as Wodehouse's villa had no piano, off trooped the three partners to the local casino, where there was a piano in a corridor off one of the gambling rooms. It was there, among the clicking of the chips and the calls of croupiers, that Wodehouse and Bolton were first delighted to hear Porter play for them "Anything Goes," "You're the Top" and "Blow, Gabriel, Blow."

As it happened, Wodehouse and Bolton were not the only ones to hear them. At one point the door was pushed open by a pleasantly intoxicated young American socialite who, in his befuddled state, concluded that Cole was the local house pianist. "Don't play that stuff, buddy," he said. "Play something *good*. Do you know a number called 'I Wonder Where My Baby is Tonight'?" Cole *did* know 'I Wonder Where My Baby is Tonight' and played it through without protest. The visitor began to cry. "That song hits me right here," he said. "Just been divorced, so can you blame me for wondering?" The three partners made sympathetic noises and Cole played 'You're the Top.' The intruder came weaving back. "Forget that stuff. Do you know a number called 'The Horse With the Lavender Eyes?' It drove us from the Plaza down to the church. Dawn said the horse had lavender eyes. Dawn O'Day—that was her stage name. Pretty isn't it?" He rose and laid a small colum of 100 franc chips on top of the piano. "What's that for?" it was asked. "For him," the drunk said, indicating Cole. "He plays O.K. but he picks out rotten numbers."

(*As he exits* U.S.C. *spot* S.C. *fades. Cross-fade to lights on half-level* S.L. *area into which* SOLO FEMALE SINGER *enters.* PROJEC- TIONS: *Fade poster and bring up abstract coloured slide behind.* BAND *have segued into intro. to "I get a Kick."*)

I GET A KICK OUT OF YOU

Verse

My story is much too sad to be told,
But practically everything leaves me totally cold.
The only exception I know is the case
When I'm out on a quiet spree,
Fighting vainly the old ennui.
Then I suddenly turn and see
Your fabulous face . . .
  (*She moves down steps to sit on half-level* S.L. *LIGHTS narrow to pin spot on her.*)

Refrain

I get no kick from champagne,
Mere alcohol doesn't thrill me at all,
So tell me, why should it be true
That I get a kick out of you?
Some get a kick from cocaine,
I'm sure that if
I took even one sniff
That would bore me terrific'lly too,
Yet I get a kick out of you.
I get a kick ev'ry time I see
You standing there before me,
I get a kick tho' it's clear to see
You obviously don't adore me
I get no kick in a plane,
Flying too high
With some guy
In the sky
Is my idea

Of nothing to do,
Yet I get a kick,
Such a fabulous kick,
Yes, I get a kick—out of you.

(LIGHTS fade on her. She remains on. PROJECTIONS: Fade screen to black. LIGHTS: Cross-fade to spot s.r. half-level into which MALE NARRATOR comes.)

NARRATOR. Listen to the sentiments of the musical theatre in the 1930s and you hear a world turning away from life. The flagpole sitters have all gone home, the girls with bobbed hair are voting for Roosevelt, radio and transatlantic fliers are old hat. But there were still diversions just as frivolous. At a time of desperate challenges at home and anxieties abroad, everybody was offering universal panaceas . . .

(LIGHTS: Blue light fills screen. General cover s.c. GIRL from "I Get A Kick" rises, comes down steps s.l. to s.c. to begin "Tomorrow." Fade NARRATOR's spot. He remains on.)

TOMORROW

GIRL.
Ladies and gentlemen, when my heart is sick,
I've got a remedy that does the trick,
So ladies and gentlemen, whenever you're blue,
I advise you to try my remedy too.
Just say—

Tomorrow, your troubles'll be done,
Tomorrow, your victory'll be won,
Tomorrow, we're all gonna have fun,
'Cause there ain't gonna be no sorrow, tomorrow.

(COMPANY in separate groups begin to appear from back get-on steps on to top-level and split into positions over various levels of the set.)

COMPANY.
Yes, yes tomorrow it's all gonna be grand,
Tomorrow, you'll start leading the band,

Tomorrow, we'll live in a new land
'Cause there ain't gonna be no sorrow, tomorrow.
There ain't gonna be
No tears in your eyes,
You ain't gonna see
No clouds in the skies,
You ain't gonna have
No worries at all,
So why do you fret and make yourself iller?
You'll feel like a killer-diller
Tomorrow, you'll wake up and feel swell,
Tomorrow, you'll start ringing the bell,
Tomorrow, we're all gonna raise hell
'Cause there ain't gonna be no sorrow—

(*FREEZE in positions.* BAND *breaks.* LIGHTS *plunge in silhouette on* COMPANY *except spot on* NARRATOR. S.L. *half-level.*)

NARRATOR. One October morning in 1938, Cole Porter, weekending in Locust Valley, Long Island, organized a riding party and chose for his own mount a difficult, nervy horse. Only a few minutes after the party rode out Porter's horse shied and fell back, crushing both his legs. In the next twenty-seven years, Porter was to endure over thirty operations and from the time of his accident until his death to enjoy scarcely a day free of pain . . .

(*LIGHTS: Fade* NARRATOR'S *spot.* COMPANY *still in silhouette as they take up "Tomorrow" again, initially very slowly then into a more threatening martial tempo for middle of the refrain and building to Accelerando finish. LIGHTS: gradually build into general cover. PROJECTIONS: Slowly bring up shot of CP playing score of show to "Leave it To Me" Company* [*in Kimball's "Cole"*] *Fade it before end of song.* COMPANY *in course of martial middle of refrain begin to come down steps to join solo girl* S.C. *into formation* S.C.)

Tomorrow there'll be nothing but peace,
Tomorrow, we'll all get a new lease,
Tomorrow, your troubles'll all cease,
'Cause there ain't gonna be no sorrow, tomorrow.
Yes, yes, tomorrow, the soldiers and their kits
Tomorrow, will put war on the fritz,

Tomorrow, and move into the Ritz
'Cause there ain't gonna be no sorrow, tomorrow.
There ain't gonna be
No tears in your eyes,
You ain't gonna see
No clouds in the skies,
You ain't gonna have
No worries at all,
So why fret and make yourself iller?
You'll feel like a killer-diller
Tomorrow, you'll wake up and feel swell,
Tomorrow, you'll start ringing the bell,
Tomorrow, we're all gonna raise hell—
Ladies and gentlemen, when my heart is sick,
I've got a remedy that does the trick,
And there ain't gonna be no sorrow—TOMORROW!

(*They advance towards audience on last bars, then wheel round and exit* U.S.C. *PROJECTIONS: Wipe screen to black and bring up Cole Porter signature across screen as LIGHTS FADE so only signature seen.*)

END OF PART ONE

PART TWO

F) WHAT IS THIS THING CALLED LOVE?

(Before House-Lights fade, BAND *on.* ENT'RACTE: BEGIN THE BEGUINE. *As house-lights fade,* COMPANY *begin to enter, with hummed harmony to final chorus of "Begin the Beguine." Bar-piece from under rostrum* S.L. *is out. Glasses, decanters, cigarettes etc. on it.* COMPANY *enter in singles and pairs, pick up glasses, cigarettes etc. Form various groups all over various stage-levels. PROJECTIONS: No specific projections in this sequence. Signature projection which has remained on screen through intermission, fades during Ent'racte. Gradually bring up master slide-collage of black-and-white Porter sheet music of love-songs. This is superimposed throughout sequence by different colours and shapes. These mood-changes should be handled as unobtrusively as possible. As "Begin the Beguine" ends,* SOLO GIRL *wanders over, glass in hand, to piano and stops in spot beside piano* S.R. *Segue into "What is this Thing?")*

WHAT IS THIS THING CALLED LOVE? (SOLO GIRL)

What is this thing called love?
This funny thing called love . . . ?

(Segue into "You do something to Me" as LIGHTS build to more general cover over floor-level S.C. YOUNG MAN *comes down steps* S.R. *towards* GIRL *who leaves bar to come down* S.C.*)*

YOU DO SOMETHING TO ME

HE.
I was mighty blue,
Thought my life was through,
Then the heavens opened
And I gazed at you.
Won't you tell me, dear
Why, when you appear,
Something happens to me
And the strangest feeling goes through me?

(*Into up-tempo chorus.*)

SHE.
You do something to me,
Something that simply mystifies me.
Tell me, why should it be
You have the pow'r to hypnotise me?
Let me live 'neath your spell,
Do do that voodoo that you do so well,
For you do something to me
That nobody else can do.

(*DANCE BREAK.*)

BOTH.
Let me live 'neath your spell,
Do do that voodoo that you do so well,
For you do something to me
That nobody else can do.

(*At end of number, she spins over towards* MAN *near pinao* S.R. *and takes his glass from him and moves again over* L. *Boy moves away* U.S. *towards bar. Man beside piano comes towards her.* BAND *segues directly into "You've Got that Thing"* [*sung and danced*].)

YOU'VE GOT THAT THING (MALE SINGER/DUET DANCE)

Verse

Since first you blew in like a boisterous breeze,
I often have wondered, dear,
Why gentlemen all seem to fall on their knees
The moment that you appear.
Your fetching physique
Is hardly unique.
You're mentally not so hot.
You'll never win laurels
Because of your morals,
But I'll tell you what you've got.

Refrain 1 (DANCE BEGINS.)

You've got that thing, you've got that thing,
That thing that makes birds forget to sing,

You've got that thing, that certain thing.
You've got that charm, that subtle charm
That makes young farmers desert the farm
'Cos you've got that thing, that certain thing.
You've got what Adam craved when he
With love for Eve was tortured;
She only had an apple tree,
But you, you've got an orchard.
You've got those ways,
Those taking ways,
That make me rush off to Cartiers,
For a wedding ring,
'Cos you've got that thing.

Refrain 2

You've got that thing, you've got that thing,
The thing that makes vines prefer to cling,
You've got that thing, that certain thing.
You've got that smile, that smile that warms,
That makes reformers reform reforms,
You've got that thing, that certain thing.
Just what made Samson be, for years
Delilah's lord and keeper?
She only had a pair of shears
But you, you've got a reaper.
You've got that pow'r, that pow'r to grip,
That makes me map out a wedding trip
For the early spring
'Cos you've got that thing.

(*They dance* U.S. *together.* ANOTHER MAN *beside bar, who's been eyeing* GIRL *on her own sitting on steps* D.S.L. *now approaches this* GIRL. *As he begins to woo her, she moves over* S.C. *and he pursues her.* BAND: *Direct segue into "Let's Misbehave."*)

LET'S MISBEHAVE (SOLO MALE)

Verse

You could have a great career,
And you should,
Only one thing stops you, dear,
You're too good.

If you want a future, darling,
Why don't you get a past?
'Cos that fatal moment's coming
At last.

Refrain

We're all alone,
No chaperone
Can get our number.
The world's in slumber,
Let's misbehave.
There's something wild
About you, child
That's so contagious,
Let's be outrageous,
Let's misbehave.
You know my heart is true
And you say, you for me care.
Somebody's sure to tell,
But what the—heck
Do we care?
They say that bears
Have love affairs,
And even camels,
We're merely mammals,
Let's misbehave.

(*She continues to be aloof. Music into frantic sub-rock beat.*)

They say that spring
Means just one thing
To little love birds,
We're not above birds,
Let's misbehave.
It's getting late
And while I wait,
My poor heart aches on.
Why keep the brakes on?
Let's misbehave.

(*Big finish, ending with* MAN *clasping her in Valentino-embrace. She sings out to audience as* BAND *segue into "Laziest Gal."*)

THE LAZIEST GAL IN TOWN

Verse

I've a beau,
His name is Jim,
He loves me
And I love him.
But he tells me I'm too prim,
That means I'm too slow.
I let him rant, I let him rave,
I let him muss my permament wave,
But when he says . . .
   MAN.
Let's misbehave.

. . . my reply is "No!"

(SHE *pushes him away. Turns to audience. NOTE: Chorus of "Laziest Gal" must NOT be over-illustrated or moved around overmuch.*)

Refrain

It's not 'cause I wouldn't,
It's not 'cause I shouldn't,
And Lord knows, it's not 'cause I couldn't,
It's simply because I'm the laziest gal in town.
My poor heart is achin'
To bring home the bacon,
And if I'm alone and forsaken,
It's simply because I'm the laziest gal in town.
Though I'm more than willing to learn
How those gals get money to burn,
Ev'ry proposition I turn down,
'Way down.
It's not 'cause I wouldn't,
It's not 'cause I shouldn't,
And Lord knows, it's not 'cause I couldn't,
It's simply because I'm the laziest gal in town.

(SHE *glides languidly over* S.L. *to resume former position on steps* D.S.L. MAN *from "Let's Misbehave" beside piano leads* BAND *into up-tempo intro. for swing version of* AT LONG LAST

LOVE. *During number,* COMPANY *in couples dance on various levels.* MAN *singing briefly dances floor-level with girl then leaps on to bar during song and at end, jumps off bar to join the "Laziest Gal" singer* D.S.L.)

AT LONG LAST LOVE

Is it an earthquake or simply a shock?
Is it the good turtle soup or merely the mock?
Is it a cocktail, this feeling of joy?
Or is what I feel the real McCoy?
Is it for all time, or merely a lark?
Is it Granada I see or merely Ashbury Park?
Is it a fancy not worth thinking of?
Or is it at long last love?
Have I the right hunch or have I the wrong?
Is it Bach that I hear or just a Cole Porter song?
Is it a fancy not worth thinking of?
Or is it at long last—at long last—love?

(*At end of number,* COMPANY *again in various groups on levels.* OLDER MAN *is behind bar and* WOMAN *beside bar. As* BAND *segue into "De-Lovely,"* MAN *begins to sing:*)

IT'S DE-LOVELY

HE.
I feel a sudden urge to sing,
The kind of ditty that invokes the spring,
So control your desire to curse
While I crucify the verse.
SHE.
This verse you've started seems to me
The Tin-Pantithesis of melody,
So spare me, please, the pain,
Just skip the darn thing and sing the refrain.
HE.
Mi, mi, mi, mi,
Re, re, re, re,
Do, sol, mi, do, la si . . .
SHE. (*Crossing to* S.C. *and motioning to* BAND.) Take it away!

(*He moves* D.S. *to her. This number moves gently over* S.C. *during following choruses.*)

HE.
The night is young, the skies are clear,
So if you want to go walking, dear,
It's delightful, it's delicious, it's de-lovely.
SHE.
I understand the reason why
You're sentimental, 'cos so am I,
It's delightful, it's delicious, it's de-lovely.
You can tell at a glance
What a swell night this is for romance,
You can hear dear Mother Nature murmuring low,
"Let yourself go!"
HE.
So please be sweet, my chickadee,
And when I kiss you, just say to me . . .

(*He plants kisses up her arm on each adjective of next few lines reaching her cheek just before "de-limit."*)

SHE.
It's delightful, it's delicious,
It's delectable, it's delirious,
It's dilemma, it's de-luxe,
It's de-limit!
    (*Smacks his hand away off her shoulder.*)
It's de-lovely!
HE.
Time marches on and soon it's plain,
You've won my heart and I've lost my brain,
It's delightful, it's delicious, it's de-lovely.
SHE.
Life seems so sweet that we decide
It's in the bag to get unified,
It's delightful, it's delicious, it's de-lovely!
BOTH.
See the crowd in that church,
See the proud parson plopped on his perch,
Get the sweet beat of that organ sealing our doom,
Here goes the groom, boom!

How they cheer and how they smile
As we go galloping down the aisle.
   SHE.
It's divine, dear.
   HE.
It's deveen, dear.
   SHE.
It's de-vallop,
   HE.
It's de-vinner,
   SHE.
It's de-voiks.
   BOTH.
It's de-lovely!

We settle down as man and wife,
To solve the riddle called "Married Life."
It's delightful, it's delicious, it's de-lovely.
We're on a crest, we have no cares,
We're just a couple of honey bears,
   SHE.
It's delightful, it's delicious, it's de-lovely.
   (*Operatic trill.*)
All's as right as can be
Till one night, at my window I see,
An absurd bird with a bundle hung on his nose—
   COMPANY.
Get baby cloes!
   SHE.
Those eyes of yours are filled with joy,
When Nurse appears and cries:

   (GIRL *comes forward with rag-doll and gives it to* MAN.)

   GIRL.
It's a boy! (*She goes back* U.S.)
   HE.
He's appalling!
   SHE.
He's appealing! (*Tug-of-war with doll.*)
   HE.
He's a polywog,

SHE.
He's a paragon!
HE.
He's a panic! He's a Pop-eye!
SHE.
He's a pip!
BOTH.
He's de-lovely!

(*She throws doll to him as they separate. He goes back to bar. She over to steps half-level* S.R. *Long intro. to "In The Still of The Night."* SOLO GIRL *goes up steps* L. *to top-level centre. LIGHTS to blue with company in shadows and spot on solo girl.*)

IN THE STILL OF THE NIGHT (SOLO FEMALE)

In the still of the night,
As I gaze from my window
At the moon in its flight,
My thoughts all stray to you.
In the still of the night,
While the world is in slumber,
Oh, the times without number
Darling, when I say to you—
"Do you love me, as I love you?
Are you my life to be, my dream come true?"
Or will this dream of mine
Fade out of sight,
Like the moon
Growing dim
On the rim
Of the hill
In the chill
Still
Of the night?
In the still of the night.

(*LIGHTS fade on* GIRL. *Cross-fade, with* BAND *segue into "I Worship You," on the spot on* MALE SINGER *on steps below half-level* S.R.)

I WORSHIP YOU (Solo Male)

Verse

Back in the days when Greece was mighty,
Men used to worship Aphrodite,
When the Phoenicians threw a party,
The driest host drank a toast to Astarte.
The big Egyptian sacrifices
Were made to please the goddess Isis,
And one of my most ancient vices
Is my worship of you.

Refrain

I don't love you, dear,
I swear it's true,
I don't love you, dear,
I worship you.
Must I modify
My point of view?
Why should I be odd if I
Worship you?
On that sacred day
When you become mine,
Somewhere, far away
I'll build you a shrine.
There I'll put you dear,
And when I do,
I'll get on my knees
And worship you.

(*LIGHTS fade on* MALE SINGER. *Spot up on* GIRL *beside piano who has sung "What Is This Thing Called Love?" previously. A glass is in her hand.*)

MAKE IT ANOTHER OLD-FASHIONED, PLEASE
(Solo Female)

Verse

Since I went on the wagon I'm
Certain drink is a major crime,
For when you lay off the liquor
You feel so much slicker,

Well, that is most of the time.
But there are moments
Sooner or later
When it's tough, I've got to say
Not to say
"Waiter!" . . .
   (*LIGHTS: up on bar.* MAN *behind as* WAITER. *She crosses to bar.*)

Refrain 1

Make it another Old-Fashioned, please,
Make it another double Old-Fashioned, please,
Make it for one who's due
To join the disillusioned crew,
Make it for one of love's new
Refugees.
Once, high in my castle I reigned supreme,
And oh! what a castle, built on a heavenly dream,
Then quick as a lightning flash,
That castle began to crash,
So make it another Old-Fashioned, please.

  SHE. Hey, Barman, what's the time?
  BARMAN. It's a quarter to three . . .
  SHE. In that case, you'd better . . .

Make it another Old-Fashioned, please,
Make it another double Old-Fashioned, please,
Make it for one who's due
To join the disillusioned crew,
Make it for one of love's new
Refugees.
Once I owned a treasure so rare, so pure,
The greatest of treasures, happiness safe and secure,
But like ev'ry hope too rash,
My treasure I find is trash,
So make it another Old-Fashioned, please.
   (SHE *motions to* BARMAN *as he makes drink.*)
Leave out the cherry,
Leave out the orange,
Leave out the bitters,
And make it—make it, make it, make it,
Just make it a straight rye!

(SHE *drinks. Then begins to move over* S.R. *and addresses* M.D.)

SHE. Hey, Mr Piano Player, why don't you play something classy?

(PIANIST *plays Mozart* [*Intro. to "Sonata In C"*].)

SHE. I like it!

(PIANO *segues into minuet-intro to "Most Gentlemen."* FEMALE SINGER *who has sung "De-Lovely" previously comes into spot centre as "Old-Fashioned" singer gets to piano.* COMPANY *generally rearrange themselves during this.*)

MOST GENTLEMEN DON'T LIKE LOVE

Solo verse

When Mummy in her sixteenth year,
Was dreaming of romance a lot,
She thought that she was Guinevere
And ev'ry boy Sir Lancelot.
But now that Mummy's more mature
And knows her way about,
She doesn't believe in "Vive l'amour,"
For Mummy's found out . . .
  (TWO OTHER GIRLS [*one from "Old Fashioned," one from "Still of the Night"*] *come to either side of her. Big cheese-cake smile, then turn to audience. Choruses get the full Andrews-Sisters' treatment.*)

Refrain 1

Most gentlemen don't like love, they just like to kick it around
Most gentlemen don't like love,
'Cos most gentlemen can't be profound.
As Madam Sappho in some sonnet said,
A slap and a tickle
Is all that the fickle
Male
Ever has in his head.
'Cos most gentlemen don't like love,
I've been in love,

So I know what I'm talking of,
And oh, to my woe I have found,
They just like to kick it around.

Refrain 2

Most gentlemen don't like love,
They just like to kick it around,
Most gentlemen can't take love,
'Cos most gentlemen can't be profound.
In ev'ry land, children, they're all the same,
A pounce in the clover,
And then when it's over,
"So long and what was your name?"
For most gentlemen don't like love,
I've been in love,
So I know what I'm talking of,
And oh, to my woe I have found,
They just like to kick it around—wah-ooo!

(TRIO *turn to face* U.S. COMPANY *begin to re-group in pairs*.)

   COMPANY.
Old love, new love,
Ev'ry love but true love . . .

(COMPANY *in pairs on various levels.* BAND *segue into "It's All Right With Me."* COMPANY *moving over and around stage during it.* [*Good point to collect glasses back on to bar*].)

IT'S ALL RIGHT WITH ME (COMPANY)

   GIRLS. (*With male harmony.*)
It's the wrong time and the wrong place,
Though your face is charming it's the wrong face,
It's not his face, but such a charming face
That it's all right with me.
   MEN. (*With female harmony.*)
It's the wrong song in the wrong style,
Though your smile is lovely, it's the wrong smile,
It's not her smile, but such a lovely smile
That it's all right with me.

GIRLS.
You can't know how happy I am that we met,
I'm strangely attracted to you.
MEN.
There's someone I'm trying so hard to forget,
Don't you want to forget someone too?
GIRLS.
It's the wrong game with the wrong chips,
MEN.
Though your lips are tempting, they're the wrong lips,
They're not her lips . . .
ALL.
But they're such tempting lips,
That if some night you're free,
Dear it's all right,
It's all right,
It's all right with me.

(*LIGHTS change to* COUPLE *behind bar.*)

FROM THIS MOMENT ON

From this moment on,
You for me, dear,
Only two for tea, dear,
From this moment on.

From this happy day,
No more blue songs,
Only whoop-dee-doo songs,
From this moment on.

For you've got the love I need so much,
Got the skin I love to touch,
Got the arms to hold me tight,
Got the sweet lips to kiss me good-night,

From this moment on,
You and I, babe,
We'll be ridin' high, babe,
Ev'ry care is gone,
From this moment on.

JUST ONE OF THOSE THINGS

SHE.
It was just one of those things,
Just one of those crazy things,
One of those bells that now and then rings,
Just one of those things.
　HE.
It was just one of those nights,
Just one of those fabulous flights,
A trip to the moon on gossamer wings,
Just one of those things.
　BOTH.
If we'd thought a bit
Of the end of it
When we started painting the town,
We'd have been aware
That our love affair
Was too hot not to cool down.

(*The* COUPLE *begin to separate.* SHE *goes* U.S.C. *and he stays at bar.*)

So, goodbye dear, and amen,
Here's hoping we meet now and then,
It was great fun
But it was just one of those things . . .

(*Direct segue into "We Shall Never Be Younger."* COUPLE *sitting on half-level steps* S.R. *LIGHTS cross-fade to them.* COMPANY *around them all over stage in silhouette.*)

WE SHALL NEVER BE YOUNGER (Duet)

We shall never be younger,
Father Time goes gaily ticking along,
We shall never be younger,
Soon the spring will tire of singing her song.
So why let love die of hunger?
We shall never be younger
Than we are today.

(*PROJECTIONS: Back to original b-and-w master-slide of music.* COMPANY *beginning to go off slowly as* BAND *segue into last of link-song. "What Is This Thing Called Love?"*)

WHAT IS THIS THING CALLED LOVE? (*Reprise*)

That's why I ask the Lord
In Heaven above,
What is this thing called love?

(COMPANY *exit. Trailing held last note. Fade to* B.O. *Screen to black. PROJECTIONS: to Hollywood Montage. LIGHTS: Spot on* NARRATOR S.L.)

NARRATOR.
In December 1935, Porter went where too many good Americans go until they die—to Hollywood. Till now his relationship with talking, or rather singing, pictures had been no more than a mild flirtation. But after Irving Berlin, Rodgers and Hart, George and Ira Gershwin had all succumbed, in 1935 Porter went out to live on the West Coast—if you can call that living. When asked by the columnists what he thought of Hollywood, his stock reply was that it was rather like living on the moon. Typically paradoxical, the sophisticated New York sybarite at first revelled in this garish world of swimming-pool parties and Polo Lounge gossip, affecting loud checked jackets and taking a mischievous pleasure in writing lush and sentimental ballads which made Louis B Mayer cry. But the crazy world of movie-making, with its excesses, expensive delays, conferences, rewrites and tantrums, not to mention the way the studios mutilated his original show-scores, could not hold him for long. There were occasional trips out West later, when offers too lucratively attractive for even Porter to refuse came along, and still there were tantrums—Judy Garland refused to sing the comedy duet in THE PIRATE—but was eventually persuaded to do so by her co-star Gene Kelly.

(*BLACKOUT. Screen to black too. Circus music over. LIGHTS. Two spots floor-level* S.C. DUO *for "Be a Clown" cross-legged on floor. This is a number which builds into a dance number, using lots of Clown props and sight-gags. PROJECTIONS: Circus ring and audience.*)

BE A CLOWN

Verse

I'll remember forever
When I was but three,

Mama, who was clever
Remarkin' to me,
If son when you're grown up
You want ev'rything nice,
I've got your future sewn up
If you take this advice . . .
   (*LIGHTS: more general cover.*)

Refrain 1

Be a clown, be a clown,
All the world loves a clown,
Act the fool, play the calf,
And you'll always have the last laugh.
Wear the cap and the bells,
And you'll rate with all the great swells,
If you become a doctor, folks'll face you with dread,
If you become a dentist, they'll be glad when you're dead,
You'll get a bigger hand if you can stand on your head,
Be a clown, be a clown, be a clown.

Refrain 2

Be a clown, be a clown,
All the world loves a clown,
If you just make 'em roar,
Watch your mountebank account soar,
Wear a painted moustache,
And you're sure to make a big splash,
A college education I should never propose,
A bachelor's degree won't even keep you in clo'es,
But millions you will win if you can spin on your nose,
Be a clown, be a clown, be a clown.

Refrain 3

Be a clown, be a clown,
All the world loves a clown,
Show 'em tricks, tell 'em jokes,
And you'll only stop with top folks;
Be a crack jackanapes,
And they'll imitate you like apes,
Why be a great composer with your rent in arrears?
Why be a major poet and you'll owe it for years,
When crowds'll pay to giggle if you wiggle your ears,
Be a clown, be a clown, be a clown.

Refrain 4

Be a clown, be a clown,
All the world loves a clown,
Be a poor silly ass,
And you'll always travel first-class,
Give 'em quips, give 'em fun,
And they'll pay to say you're A-1,
If you become a farmer you've the weather to buck,
If you become a gambler you'll be stuck with your luck,
But Jack you'll never lack if you can quack like a duck,
(Quack, quack, quack, quack),
Be a clown, be a clown, be a clown.

(*Running exit for* Duo. BLACKOUT. *Then spot up on solo* FEMALE *on top level* S.L.)

I CONCENTRATE ON YOU

Whenever skies look grey to me
And trouble begins to brew,
Whenever the winter winds become too strong,
I concentrate on you.

When fortune cries "nay, nay!" to me
And people declare "You're through,"
Whenever the Blues become my only song,
I concentrate on you.

On your smile so sweet, so tender,
When at first your kiss I decline,
On the light in your eyes when I surrender
And once again our arms intertwine.

And so when wise men say to me
That love's young dream never comes true,
To prove that even wise men can be wrong
I concentrate on you.
I concentrate and concentrate on you.

(*LIGHTS X fade to* NARRATOR S.R. *Return to Hollywood projection.*)

NARRATOR.
One afternoon, as they sat by his Hollywood pool, Greta Garbo asked Cole if he was happy. He considered the question carefully before replying "Yes, I think I am." Her eyes swivelled to the middle distance and she sighed—"That must be very strange." Strange or not, by 1940 he was back where he was happiest—on Broadway!

H) BACK TO BROADWAY

(*LIGHTS: Fade on* NARRATOR. *Three spots on ascending levels with* THREE MALE SINGERS *in tails and top hats in separate spots* S.L. *PROJECTIONS: Cross-fade to collage of Broadway: Marquees, lights, etc.*)

PLEASE DON'T MONKEY WITH BROADWAY

Verse

Due to landscape gardeners gifted,
Father Knickerbocker's face is being lifted
So much
That you'd hardly know it as such.
All the streets are being dressed up,
So before they ruin Broadway,
I suggest up you go
To the City Fathers and say "Whoa!"
   (*They come down* S.L. *steps for dance with canes.*)

Refrain 1

Glorify Sixth Avenue,
And put bathrooms in the zoo,
But please, don't monkey with Broadway.
Put big floodlights in the park,
And put Harlem in the dark,
But please—don't monkey with Broadway.
Though it's tawdry and plain,
It's a lovely old lane,
Full of landmarks galore and memories gay,
So, move Grant's Tomb to Union Square,
And put Brooklyn anywhere,
But please, please, I beg on my knees,
Don't monkey with old Broadway.

Refrain 2

Plant trees in the Polo Grounds
And put Yorkville out of bounds,
But please—don't monkey with Broadway.
Close the Village honky-tonks,
Suppress cheering in the Bronx,
But please—don't monkey with Broadway.
Think what names used to dance
On this road of romance,
Think what stars used to stroll along it all day.
Make City Hall a skating rink,
And push Wall Street in the brink,
But please, please, I beg on my knees
Don't monkey with old Broadway.

(*They exit* D.S.L. *Overlap hot drum break as* THREE GIRLS *enter in rhythm to half-level* S.L. [*They are in black skirts, black sequinned jackets, red shoes, '40's style*].) PROJECTIONS: *Dissolve to silhouettes of band leaders superimposed on Broadway collage.*)

THE LEADER OF A BIG-TIME BAND

Verse

If a girl in any sector
Makes you feel like a puppy called Hector,
And you're longing to subject 'er,
To elect her your bride and protect 'er,
If she's just as sweet as nectar,
But of your job she's no respecter,
Become a top band director,
And you never, never will miss . . .
   (*They come to form trio-group on steps* D.S.L.)

Refrain 1

In the gilded age, a Wall Street Millionaire,
Was the answer to a working maiden's prayer,
But today she'd chuck that yearly fifty grand
For the leader of a big-time band.
When, in Venice, Georgia Sand with Chopin romped,
Her Libido had the Lido simply swamped,

But today who would be buried in the sand?
Why, the leader of a big-time band.
When Goodman, champ of champs,
Goes blowin' blue,
Rum-ridden debutramps
Nearly come to,
So, if, say you still can play a one-night stand,
Be the leader of a big-time band.

Refrain 2

When in Reno, ladies we know used to clown,
All the chaps who wore the shaps would wear 'em down,
But today the only rider they demand,
Is the leader of a big-time band.
When Salome got John the B. and by the head,
It appears he wasn't kosher in the bed,
But today who'd be the goy she'd like to land?
Why the leader of a big-time band.
   (*DANCE BREAK:* JITTERBUG *by* BOY *and* GIRL DANCER. *During it, the* TRIO *go up* S.L. *steps in rhythm to form group on top-level centre. At end of dance,* BOY *and* GIRL *run off and* TRIO *continue. NOTE: With a reduced company, and if the choreographic resources are not available, the Jitterbug break should be cut and replaced by the* TRIO *moving in rhythm to the brief dance-break music.*)
When Dorsey comes to tea
With Gypsy Rose,
She gets so het-up, she
Puts on her clo'es,
And she only turns one cheek while being scanned
By the leader of a big-time,
Dig time, jig-a-jig-a-jig time,
Band—do wah, do wah, do wah, dowaaaah!

(*Play-out music to cover their exit off top-level. LIGHTS: cross fade to spot on* NARRATOR *D.S.L. PROJECTIONS: stay the same, removing only the band-leader superimposition.*)

NARRATOR.
For a composer to write 23 shows and then come up with his masterpiece is somewhat unusual in the history of Broadway. By 1948, Porter hadn't had a hit in five years. The idea of setting Shakespeare

to music wasn't a new one. In fact, quite a number of literary works had been set to music; there had been "Show Boat," "Pal Joey," "Tales of the South Pacific"—there was even a rumour that someone was going to make a musical out of "The Desert Song." But nobody thought much of a backstage musical based on "The Taming of the Shrew"; nobody wanted to back it, the producers were young unknowns, and nobody thought it would work. Porter was regarded as too old by experts who had never been old enough. On Broadway, the general feeling was that the Cole Porter era was over . . .

(*Fade lights on* NARRATOR *who exits as* NARRATOR TWO *comes into spot* D.S.R.)

NARRATOR TWO.
In fact, the reality was taking on the shape of one of the awful scenarios that had sent him laughing from Hollywood. But as Porter knew to his own cost, bad movies always have happy endings. Finally, enough money was scraped together to put the show on. And if audiences couldn't understand "Kiss Me Kate," they'd have to do what Porter himself did when writing it—go back to the original . . .

BRUSH UP YOUR SHAKESPEARE

(*He turns and begins to go* U.S. TWO BOWERY BUMS *appear and take an arm each and run him back* D.S. *as* BAND *segue into intro to "Brush Up." PROJECTIONS: Bring up title of "Kiss Me, Kate" behind Broadway masterslide. LIGHTS: build to general cover floor—level* S.C.)

BUM 1.
The girls today, in society,
Go for classical poetry,
BUM 2.
So to win their hearts,
You must quote with ease,
Aeschylus and Euripides
BUM 1.
You must know Homer and b'lieve me, bo',
Sophocles, also Sappho-ho.
BUM 2.
Unless you know Shelley and Keats and Pope,
Dainty debbies will call you a dope.

BOTH.
But the poet of 'em all,
You will start 'em simply ravin',
Is the poet people call
The Bard of Stratford on Avon.
ALL.
Brush up your Shakespeare,
Start quoting him now,
Brush up your Shakespeare,
And the women you will wow.
TOFF.
Just declaim a few lines from "Othella,"
And they'll think you're a helluva fella,
BUM 2.
If your blonde won't respond when you flatter 'er,
Tell her what Tony told Cleopatterer.
BUM 1.
If she fights when her clo'es you are mussin',
What are clo'es? "Much Ado About Nussin',"
ALL.
Brush up your Shakespeare,
And they'll all kow-tow.
TOFF.
With the wife of the British embessida,
Try a crack out of "Troilus and Cressida."
BUM 2.
If she then wants an all to herself night,
Let her rest ev'ry 'leventh or "Twelfth Night."
BUM 1.
If she says your behaviour is heinous,
Kick her right in the "Coriolanus."
ALL.
Brush up your Shakespeare,
And they'll all kow-tow.
TOFF.
If you can't be a ham and do "Hamlet,"
Then they won't give a damn or a damlet,
BUM 2.
Just recite an occasional sonnet
And your lap'll have "Honey" upon it,
BUM 1.
When your baby is pleadin' for pleasure,
Let her sample your "Measure for Measure,"

ALL.
Brush up your Shakespeare,
And they'll all kow-tow.
TOFF.
Better mention "The Merchant of Venice"
When her sweet pound of flesh you would menace,
BUM 2.
If her virture at first she defends, well
Just remind her that "All's Well That Ends Well."
BUM 1.
And if still she won't give you a bonus,
You know what Venus got from Adonis!
ALL.
Brush up your Shakespeare,
And they'll all kow-tow.

Brush up your Shakespeare,
Start quoting him now,
Brush up your Shakespeare,
And the women you will wow.
(GIRL SINGER *appears in shadows on half-level* S.L.)
So tonight just recite to your matey
(*They turn to* GIRL.)
TOFF.
"Kiss me Kate"
BUM 1.
"Kiss Me, Kate"
BUM 2.
"Kiss me Katey."
ALL.
Brush up your Shakespeare,
And they'll all kow-tow.
And they'll all kow-tow.
TOFF.
I trow!
ALL.
And they'll all kow-tow.
TOFF.
Forsooth!
ALL.
And they'll all kowtow.

TOFF.
Gadzooks!
ALL.
And they'll all kowtow!

(*They exit in chain* U.S. *During applause, LIGHTS fade to bluish spot half-level* S.L. GIRL SINGER 1 *moves into it. PROJECTIONS: KEEP "Kate" title. Dim it slightly. She looks after exiting men, then turns.*)

WHY CAN'T YOU BEHAVE?

GIRL 1.
Why can't you behave?
Oh, why can't you behave?
After all the things you told me,
And the promises that you gave,
Oh, why can't you behave?

(GIRL 2 *comes into spot half-level* S.R.)

GIRL 2.
Why can't you be good,
And do just as you should?
Won't you turn that new leaf over
So your baby can be your slave?
Oh, why can't you behave?

(GIRL 3 *comes into spot top-level centre.*)

GIRL 3.
There's a farm I know near my old home-town,
Where we two can go and try settlin' down.
There I'll care for you forever,
Well, at least till they dig my grave,
Oh, why can't you behave?

(*They begin to come down from levels to floor-level, to exit* U.S.C., *singing as they move. Fade spots and build to dim light* S.C. *area:*)

ALL.
Why can't you behave?
Oh, why can't you behave?
After all the things you told me,
And the promises that you gave,
Oh why can't you behave?

(*Long last note held offstage.* NARRATOR *enters just as note dies away on top level* L. *PROJECTIONS: Fade screens to black. During following speech and song, PROJECTIONS dissolve through six pictures of* PORTER, *starting with last picture taken, moving back in time through picture of CP at piano, CP after accident entering theatre, CP at Worcester Academy, ending with early picture of young CP in straw boater filling screen. LIGHTS: Cross-fade to spot on* NARRATOR.)

NARRATOR.
"Kiss Me, Kate" was a happy experience, but it wasn't quite the happy ending. Porter was to continue to write and compose for another ten years, always in pain and always uncomplaining about it. His whole life had been lived in the demanding glare of other people's admiration—first, his mother, then his college friends, the Paris crowd, Broadway, Hollywood—the whole literate, civilised world. By the '50s, that world was changing. Paris was yesterday, the cafe society of the between-the-war years had faded from the scene. Broadway too had changed from the free and easy days when anything went. Now the money men, the producers and their accountants called the tune. In 1948 he was back on top, and in 1958 he wrote the last Cole Porter song, in which he tried to imagine a condition of life he had never known . . .

(PIANO *begins "WOULDN'T IT BE FUN?" reprise and* NARRATOR *talk-sings opening lines of it before singing the ending very quietly:*)
Wouldn't it be fun not to be famous?
Wouldn't it be fun not to be rich?
Wouldn't it be pleasant to be a simple peasant
And spend a happy day digging a ditch?
Wouldn't it be fun not to be known as
An important VIP?
Wouldn't it be fun to be nearly anyone
Except me—mixed-up me!

COLE

(Slowly fade spot on him. SOLO FEMALE VOICE *begins "Ev'ry Time" offstage, coming on in darkness to spot top-level centre as final PROJECTION very slowly fades away.)*

EV'RY TIME WE SAY GOODBYE

SOLO.
Ev'ry time we say goodbye
I die a little,
Ev'ry time we say goodbye
I wonder why a little,
Why the gods above me
Who must be in the know
Think so little of me,
They allow you to go.

*(*COMPANY *on in darkness, over various levels, to join in chorale-setting for rest of number. LIGHTS: gradually build but kept dim.)*

COMPANY.
When you're near,
There's such an air of Spring about it,
I can hear
A lark somewhere begin to sing about it,
There's no love song finer,
But how strange the change
From major to minor,
Ev'ry time we say goodbye,
Ev're single time we say goodbye.

(As last note is held, "Cole Porter" signature comes up on screen. LIGHTS: Fade slowly on COMPANY. *Then PROJECTIONS: Fade signature to synchronise. BLACKOUT.)*

THE END

PRODUCTION NOTE

COLE was originally produced with a cast of ten (five male, five female). For stock and amateur productions it would be possible to produce the show with a slightly smaller cast, which would necessitate only some slight redistribution of material, although the company numbers (such as "Another Openin', Another Show," "Anything Goes," "Tomorrow," etc) might suffer in impact with anything less than a cast of six.

In the original Mermaid production, the set consisted of a highly-polished squared black floor, with a multi-levelled flight of steps at each side leading to a central high bridge-level Upstage, behind which was the back-projection screen. The original production used a constant series of changing images on the projection screen, the most important of which are indicated in this edition, but obviously if the resources for complex back-projection are not available, it would be better to rely on abstract images conveyed by lighting and perhaps using slides only for the most important photographic images.

The band at the Mermaid was placed Stage Right with the grand piano on floor level and the other musicians arranged in an Art-Deco style—bandstand on two tiers. There was a useful multiplicity of exits and entrances (necessary with so many quick changes) from each side, from both sides underneath the central bridge, from steps S.R. and S.L. on to the central bridge, and up steps from behind the back-projection screen on to the central bridge. One other useful setting-piece was a moveable rostrum concealed underneath the S.L. steps which could be pulled out to represent the catwalk in "Come On In" and the important focal point of the bar in the love-song sequence.

Although settings will inevitably vary in degrees of elaboration, some effort to provide differing performing levels is recommended. This facilitates the continuous flow of the entertainment, which works best when it avoids the cabaret-style presentation of a series of separate numbers: for instance, it is also advisable to avoid breaking the momentum of the show with too many breaks for applause after individual items. In the love-song sequence, it was found that this worked at its best when the rest of the cast focused on each performer in turn, helping the sense of a continuous party and also joining in applause if and when it occurred—it is important that this sequence in particular communicates an atmosphere of sophisticated fun.

It may also be worth pointing out that although the original production had a constant variety of pace and effective changes of both lighting and projection as the action moved between different stage levels, it tried to avoid over-elaboration of the numbers. Apart from the Jazz Ballet from "Within The Quota" and the contribution of the same performer (a skilled dancer) to company numbers and "Be A Clown," the choreography was deliberately unfussy, the essential emphasis always being on the clarity and projection of the lyrics.

Finally, it should be stressed that COLE can only be performed in the format presented here as approved by the Mermaid Theatre and Cole Porter Musical and Literary Property Trusts, and under no circumstances may there be any alteration in the running order, change or substitution of other Cole Porter material.

ALAN STRACHAN

DESIGNER'S NOTES AND NOTES ON SLIDES

1. The set, consisted basically of two flights of steps linked by a bridge upstage, with a highly polished squared black floor. In addition to facilitating the flow of the action, its purpose was to invoke an emotional view of New York—an intimation of skyscrapers and patterns of bright lights. It was simply conceived in order to be stylish and elegant—to represent the period without being an academic reproduction of period style. Flexibility, too, was very important, and numerous exits and entrances were incorporated into the design.

2. In keeping with the idea of a dateless elegance, which still reflected the period of Porter's greatest fame, costumes were designed to be as basic and as elegant as possible. The women all had one long, very simply cut evening gown, in tones of grey and black, and a "day" outfit of white, consisting of a skirt and jacket, which could be altered with various accessories for different numbers. The men had suits of tails (black and grey) and white suits, which could also be altered by adding various accessories. More extravagant costumes were used in some of the speciality numbers; i.e. LOST LIBERTY BLUES, LEADER OF A BIG TIME BAND, and BE A CLOWN.

SLIDES

1. In the original production slides were used to illustrate the text and to make Cole Porter and his life more immediate to both the cast and the audience. But in no way was this a "lantern slide show." The idea was to provide a kinetic background to enhance and illuminate the production. We used three pairs of cross-fading Kodak carousel projectors, placed behind the screen. This allowed for quick and smooth changing of the slides, and each pair of projectors covered one third of the screen area with slight overlap.

2. Some of the slides, but not all of them, called for will be available in the future on a rental basis. WRITE for details.

PETER DOCHERTY

ARRANGER'S NOTES

With the orchestrations available, the following combinations can be used:

1. PIANO
   BASS
   DRUMS

2. PIANO
   BASS
   DRUMS
   ALTO SAXOPHONE DOUBLING FLUTE AND CLARINET

3. TWO PIANOS, USING TWO SETS OF PIANO PARTS AND TWO PIANISTS CAPABLE OF IMPROVISING BETWEEN THEMSELVES.

KEN MOULE

NOTES ON BIOGRAPHIES

BERNARD MILES, co-founder and artistic director of the Mermaid Theatre with his wife, Josephine Wilson, has had a long and distinguished career on stage, film, television and radio. His 40 years experience in the theatre as actor, director, electrician, property master and carpenter led inevitably to the building of the original Mermaid Theatre in the back garden of his London home in 1951. The move to a converted warehouse on the banks of the Thames at Blackfriars took place in 1959 when the Mermaid Theatre at Puddle Dock opened with the new musical, LOCK UP YOUR DAUGHTERS—the first time that a permanent live theatre had been in the City of London for 300 years.

The site has early theatrical connections. It is directly opposite bankside where the great theatres of Shakespeare's day once stood, and at Blackfriars itself was a small private playhouse of which Shakespeare was one of the seven shareholders.

The Mermaid was built entirely by public subscription, from the "buy-a-brick-for-half-a-crown" campaign, to larger contributions from City Livery Companies, banks, stock brokers, Trusts and Foundations. Since then, the theatre has built up an international reputation, presenting a remarkable variety of productions—musicals such as COLE, COWARDY CUSTARD and SIDE BY SIDE BY SONDHEIM, English and foreign classics, and new plays from home and abroad, as well as concerts, film shows and productions for children such as TREASURE ISLAND, and GULLIVER's TRAVELS, and the wonderful educational theatre, THE MOLECULE CLUB.

Bernard Miles was awarded the CBE in 1953, knighted in 1969 and made a life peer in 1979. (Only two actors have been so honoured in the history of the theatre.)

ALAN STRACHAN was born and educated in Scotland, and began his professional theatre career at the Mermaid Theatre in 1970. He remained at the Mermaid for five years, latterly as Associate Director; productions there included "John Bull's Other Island," "The Old Boys," "Misalliance," "Children" and he co-devised the two long-running Musical Revues "Cowardly Custard" and "Cole," also co-directing the latter. In the West End he directed two Alan Ayckbourn plays—"Confusions" and "Just Between Ourselves"—as well as "A Family and a Fortune" and "Yahoo," which he co-authored with Alec Guinness. In Amsterdam he directed the Dutch production of Ayckbourn's "Bedroom Farce" and returned to the Mermaid for the solo play "The Immortal Haydon" starring Leonard Rossiter. In 1978 he became Artistic Director of London's Greenwich Theatre, where he has directed new plays (such as "An Audience Called Edouard," and "I Sent a Letter to My Love") and revivals (such as "The Play's The Thing," "Private Lives" and "Present Laughter," the latter two of which subsequently transferred to the West End).

KEN MOULE entered the music profession in 1945 as pianist with Oscar Rabin's Band. In 1947 worked with John Dankworth and Ronnie Scott on S.S. Queen Mary. Worked with Dance Bands on tour and in night clubs for ten years, broadcasting frequently and arranging for the bands with which he played. In 1957 he formed his own jazz band, later joining Ted Heath as staff arranger for two years. He then worked abroad for a year returning to London as Musical Director in *Fings Ain't Wot They Used T' Be*. Since then he has conducted and arranged innumerable musicals and BBC radio programmes although his primary interest is still jazz. His last album was *Adam's Rib Suite*. Musical Arranger for 3 Mermaid shows: COLE, FARJEON REVUED and OH! MR PORTER.

PETER DOCHERTY, DESIGNER: Peter has designed for all forms of theatre. He has worked with many of the leading ballet companies, including the American Ballet Theatre, Scottish Ballet, Houston Ballet, Royal Ballet, London Festival Ballet and London Contemporary Dance Theatre, as well as operas in Copenhagen and London. In the theatre he has also worked at the Royal Court, and designed the original productions of COLE and SIDE BY SIDE BY SONDHEIM for the Mermaid Theatre.

BENNY GREEN: Musician and writer. Professional saxophonist, 1947–61. Appeared with every type of band from the Stan Kenton and Ronnie Scott orchestras to the Galtymore Irish Country Dance band. Began broadcasting for the BBC in 1955, since which time has written and delivered more than 2000 broadcasts, including major series on the History of Popular Music, the Development of the Hollywood Musical, the Moguls of Hollywood, and extended biographies of Ella Fitzgerald, Fred Astaire and Stanley Holloway. On television his credits include a three-part history of London for Thames TV, and documentaries on Irving Berlin, Duke Ellington and Jerome Kern. He joined The Observer as jazz critic in 1959 and remained in that post for the next nineteen years. Since 1972 he has been a regular weekly contributor to Punch, as reviewer of Cinema and TV, since 1970 a weekly book reviewer for The Spectator, since 1977 as a humorous columnist for The Daily Mirror, and since 1978 as a weekly contributor to "What's On in London."

His publications include two novels, three volumes of musical criticism, biographies of Astaire and P. G. Wodehouse, a history of comic postcards, an analysis of Bernard Shaw's involvement with prizefighting, a volume of autobiography and, as editor, three cricket anthologies. In the theatre he has written the libretto of an opera based on "Lysistrata," the new book of the revival of "Show Boat" which ran in London's West End for over 900 performances, and, apart from "Cole," a second show devoted to the same composer called "Oh, Mr Porter." Among his collaborations with musician John Dankworth is "Boots With Strawberry Jam" (1968) a musical biography of Bernard Shaw starring John Neville and Cleo Laine.

PROPERTY LIST

- 1 straw fan
- 1 brass lighter
- 10 nip glasses
- 1 red plastic fan
- 1 silver tray
- assorted glasses
- 1 tray
- 2 cocktail shakers
- 1 cigarette holder
- 1 cocktail stick holder
- 1 silver ice bucket
- 1 cherry and lemon container
- 1 gilt cigarette case
- 2 lighters
- 1 large feather fan
- 6 streamers
- 1 whistle
- assorted newspapers
- 1 red diary
- 4 suitcases
- 1 director's chair
- 2 clown's noses
- 1 bird on a wire
- 1 pack trick cards
- 2 bunches trick flowers
- 1 black make-up stick
- 1 imitation ring
- 1 floppy dolly
- 3 canes (plus 2 spares)
- 1 small fan
- imitation money
- 1 clipboard and attached pencil
- 1 USA flag
- 1 Liberty Torch
- 2 toothbrushes
- 1 ball
- 2 paint buckets
- 1 pair spectacles
- 1 wine cooler
- 1 newspaper bag
- cigar
- 2 hat boxes
- 1 wicker basket
- 2 chairs

BIOGRAPHY

COLE PORTER, one of the outstanding American composer-lyricists of the 20th century, was born in Peru, Indiana in 1891, the only son of Samuel and Kate Porter. His early life was dominated by the strong personalities of his mother, who determined he should pursue a career as a musician, and his maternal grandfather, J. O. Cole who had come to the then frontier town of Peru as a boy in 1834 and who became a rich landowner. Porter was educated at Worcester Academy, Massachusetts and then at Yale where his musical talents found ideal scope in the Glee Club and the Yale Dramat, for which he wrote several musical-comedies, as well as writing songs for the Yale football team which are still sung at Yale. Lasting college friends included Gerald Murphy (the model for Fitzgerald's Dick Diver in 'Tender is the Night') and Monty Woolley, with whom he collaborated in later work.

After Yale he began studying law at Harvard (where he roomed with Dean Acheson) at his grandfather's insistence, but later switched to music. His first produced full-scale professional work was the comic opera, 'See America First' which had a brief Broadway run in 1916. For the next twelve years, his life was spent mostly abroad. He married a rich socialite, Linda Lee Thomas, in 1919 and they travelled constantly between Paris, Venice, London and the Riviera during the 1920s.

Porter composed a jazz-ballet, 'Within The Quota,' in collaboration with Gerald Murphy in 1923, premiered by the Ballets Suédois in Paris, and wrote a revue for Les Ambassadeurs in Paris in 1928. Occasionally he placed songs in Broadway shows (including 'The Greenwich Village Follies' in 1924) and London revues for C. B. Cochran.

His Broadway career began in earnest with 'Paris' (1928) and 'Fifty Million Frenchmen' (1929), the success of which ended his expatriate period. The 1930s saw a remarkable succession of Cole Porter successes on Broadway, including 'The New Yorkers' (1930), 'Gay Divorce' with Fred Astaire (1932), 'Nymph Errant' (London only, 1933), 'Anything Goes' (1934), 'Jubilee' (1935), 'Red Hot and Blue' (1936) and 'Du Barry Was A Lady' with Ethel Merman and Bert Lahr (1939). He also worked in Hollywood in the 30s, his original film scores including 'Born To Dance' (1936) and 'Rosalie' (1937).

In 1938 he suffered a serious riding accident which dogged him for the rest of his life, but his career continued in both theatre and films. His Broadway success continued through the early 1940s with 'Panama Hattie' (1940), 'Let's Face It' (1941), and 'Something For The Boys' (1943), although both 'Seven Lively Arts' (1944) a lavish Billy Rose revue, and 'Around The World' (1946) for Orson Welles were less successful. 'Kiss Me Kate' in 1948 restored his pre-eminence as the supreme American creator of musical comedies, and his later shows included 'Out Of This World' (1950), 'Can-Can' (1953) and 'Silk Stockings' (1955).

His Hollywood work during his later career included 'The Pirate' (1948), 'High Society' (1956) and 'Les Girls' (1957). His last work was his only contribution for television—a musical version of 'Aladdin' (1958).

His health deteriorated during his last years; Cole Porter died in October, 1964 in Santa Monica, California, at the age of 73.